PELE'S PREROGATIVE

PELE'S PREROGATIVE

by Albert Tucher

ALSO BY
Albert Tucher

A Place of Refuge

The Hollow Vessel

Blood Like Rain

Honorary Jersey Girl

PELE'S PREROGATIVE

a Big Island Mystery

ALBERT TUCHER

Published by **Shotgun Honey Books**

215 Loma Road
Charleston, WV 25314
www.ShotgunHoney.com

Cover Design by Bad Fido.

ISBN-10: 1-956957-78-2
ISBN-13: 978-1-956957-78-5

10 9 8 7 6 5 4 3 2 1   25 24 23 22 21 20 19

*In loving memory of
Doris Tucher (1925-2012)
and Albert Tucher (1926-2011).*

PELE'S PREROGATIVE

1

ON HER LIST of a cop's favorite thankless tasks, Jenny Freitas ranked welfare checks somewhere in the middle—not as dangerous as domestic disputes, but not as routine as taking reports of rental car break-ins, either.

"Nobody's seen him in a week," said a relative or neighbor to start the process. "Ain't like him."

The situation usually ended with the missing person staggering home from a bender and showing zero gratitude for anyone's concern.

Langston Otsaka had that kind of record, but he was seventy-three now, and his file of assaults and drunk and disorderlies had petered out twenty years ago. If his neighbors worried about him now, they might have a point.

Jenny parked two doors away from the Otsaka address in the homelands subdivision outside Pahoa. She didn't expect gunfire to erupt from the typical whitewashed Big Island box, but cops always allowed for the possibility of ambush.

She would almost have preferred a life and death situation to what did happen. As she climbed out of her Camry, a familiar Chevy Impala pulled up behind her. Like her vehicle, the car bore a blue Hawaii County police cone on the roof.

Officer Lance Callen climbed out and gave her a leer that he probably considered an ingratiating grin. His eyes settled on her chest. Maybe someday he would surprise her, but not today.

"I'm your backup," he said.

"I didn't call for backup."

She would have welcomed the help from one of her friends on the force. But she had learned to put distance between herself and Callen since his transfer from Kona two months earlier. His kind of backup was too hands-on.

"I got this," she said.

He lost his smile.

"You turn down help when it's offered, it might not be there when you need it."

"Do you realize what you just said?"

"It's the way it is."

From Callen's car came the sound of Dispatch putting out a burglary call. The location was just five minutes away.

"You gonna get that?" Jenny asked.

She put the pressure on him with her eyes, until he broke off the staring contest and climbed back into his

Impala. He spoke into his radio and drove off. Jenny turned back to the Otsaka residence.

Nothing looked out of place. She went up and knocked on the front door, but it couldn't be that easy.

Next she made a circuit around the house. She tried peering through the windows, but Mr. Otsaka had cranked the slats shut. Jenny wondered why people did that. To her, the point of living on the gentle Hilo side of the Big Island of Hawaii was to blur the line between indoors and out. The more popular Kona side beckoned to those who wanted to bake in the sun until they sizzled and then go home and crank up the AC.

She paused in the back yard and wondered about the tingle that climbed her spine. By itself the feeling wasn't much help. She tried to empty her mind and let her senses rule.

Something about the back fence looked funny, and after a moment she saw the problem. The vegetation gripping the painted wooden slats looked lopsided, like an unfinished haircut.

She went closer and liked the analogy even better. Someone had been trimming the bushes and vines, starting on the left. Cut ends of branches and tendrils still looked raw. Jenny felt like a woodsman as she followed the fresh cuts a third of the way along the fence, until she reached the point where the horticulture stopped and the wilderness resumed. She took another step.

Where was the ground?

Interesting question, but she didn't have time for it

now. She started to topple forward. Her right foot kept testing the void, but her mind was already searching for plan B. She spun and grabbed for anything she could get. Her right hand caught the horizontal slat midway up the four-foot fence. For the moment she stopped falling. Her left hand found the base of the last trimmed bush and clung to it.

But her right foot still dangled, and now her left was sliding off the edge of the hole.

The fence was solid and the bush was holding, but the stalemate with gravity couldn't last.

The fence offered more stability than the bush. Jenny raised her left knee and groped for the jagged edge of the hole. Tomorrow her scrapes and bruises would remind her of how she had spent these desperate moments.

If there was a tomorrow. That depended on what she did now.

She mapped out the next few seconds. She had to push with her knee and grab the fence with her left hand. If she missed, her second attempt would be weaker, and her third weaker still.

But all those pull-ups in the gym paid off now, as she caught the cross-beam. With both hands on the fence, she could climb it like a ladder. When she had enough height, she planted her feet on the two-by-four that kept the bottom of the fence rigid. Then she inched to her left until she had regained solid ground.

Jenny sucked air in and blew it out. It felt so good that she did it again, and again.

Okay, she had earned the right to breathe, but now came the part about doing her job. Jenny crawled to the edge of the hole that had almost swallowed her, testing the ground with her hands as she went. It stayed solid, and soon she could peer over the edge of the gap and into the darkness below.

She took her flashlight from her belt and sent the beam downward. Ten or fifteen feet down she saw what she expected to see.

Someone's encounter with the hole had gone worse than hers.

On her hands and knees Jenny backed up until she felt confident of the ground. She got up, unhooked her radio, and called Dispatch.

"Start a bus, a detective and rescue to my location."

"What's up, Officer?"

"I just found a lava tube. It's occupied."

Jenny wanted the last two words back, but the dispatcher let her get away with her flippant response.

"En route, Officer."

That left her more than enough time to think, and to come to the inevitable conclusion. She should have accepted the offer of backup, even if it came from Callen. She hated it when things worked out like that.

• • •

Just a few hours earlier, someone popping out of the earth would have made Jenny reach for her sidearm, but a lot had changed since then.

"No rush," said the woman. "He's D.O.A."

Two of the woman's male colleagues from the Hawaii County Fire Department snagged the line she dangled from and pulled her over solid ground. The hoist operator lowered her until she landed on her feet.

"No way to tell when the skylight broke through," she said as she unhooked herself and dropped her harness to the ground.

Geologists called the thin crust over a lava tube a skylight.

"Maybe he didn't walk back here that often," said Detective Coutinho. "I'll have to tell Lucy about this the next time she gets on me about the yard work."

Jenny wanted to be Lucy Coutinho when she grew up. Any smart young woman did.

"Anything look funny about it?"

"He fell straight down. Cleanest fall I ever saw. Nothing for him to hit on the way."

Jenny winced as she thought of Otsaka's seconds of impotent terror.

"Might as well bring him out," said Coutinho.

He looked toward the waiting ambulance and then at Jenny.

"EMS has nothing to do until we get the body up. Let them check you out."

"I'm good."

He pointed at the red island mud on her knees and then at the oozing scrapes on both elbows.

"I'd say you almost joined him down there. *Tita* is good, but smart is better. Go."

Jenny wasn't worrying about her tough chick credentials. The problem was one of the EMS people, a young man named Jack Holloway. She had spent some time in his bed, and she didn't want to get personal with him right now.

Jack kept it professional as he dabbed her elbows with disinfectant, but that just made her feel worse.

His attentions distracted her from the body as it emerged on a rescue litter. The rescue team maneuvered the dead man onto a body bag laid out to receive him. Jenny tried not to wince as she took in the broken face. Coutinho was keeping it professional, and she always wanted to emulate him.

"Wait a sec," he said.

He snapped a glove onto his right hand and reached for Otsaka's left wrist. Coutinho lifted and hefted the wrist before turning his eyes toward Jenny.

"Gonna need an autopsy," he said.

Well, yeah, she thought.

An unattended death demanded one.

"No, I mean we're really gonna need an autopsy."

2

NOW COUTINHO WANTED Jenny to witness the autopsy. If she aspired to a detective assignment someday, she would have to get used to the yucky stuff. He seemed to have hopes for her, and her determination to live up to his expectations helped steady her nerves.

Dr. Ramesh looked mostly Japanese instead of Indian, but the ethnic melting pot in these islands did things like that. Jenny was basically the Portuguese brunette that her name predicted, but she also saw traces of Japanese and Filipino in her bathroom mirror.

The doctor weighed and measured the body and recording his findings. He described the perimortem bruising on the front of the body.

"Interesting," he said.

Coutinho nodded. Jenny hoped one of them would give her a hint about what they had seen.

"No wrist fractures," said Coutinho. "That's what I noticed before."

"Oh," she said.

Then the doctor and an orderly turned the body over.

"Hmm."

"Hmm is right," said Coutinho.

He turned to Jenny.

"What do you see?"

Panic flared for a moment, and her mind went blank. Coutinho waited. His patience was legendary in the department, but even he must have his limits.

"Cleanest fall I ever saw," Jenny remembered the woman rescuer saying.

"Where did that wound on the back of his head come from?" she asked.

Coutinho grinned.

"Good call. One impact from the fall. Injuries should be in one plane. On his front, judging from his face and chest. But he didn't put out his hands to catch himself. Wouldn't have done any good, but still, it's human nature."

"And something or somebody hit him on the back of the head," said Jenny.

"Unless a meteor fell out of the sky, I'm betting on somebody. Which would make it a homicide."

"Come to think of it," said Jenny, "we didn't find the tool he was using to prune the bushes."

Coutinho gave him one of his rare smiles, and the whole ordeal became worth it.

• • •

The next day Coutinho took Jenny and Office Sammy Waga, all three hundred plus pounds of him, to search Otsaka's house. Jenny always enjoyed Sammy's grumpiness and his indifference to her sex. Some of her other male colleagues could learn from him.

"What do we know?" Coutinho asked.

"The neighbor who called the welfare check in said he lived alone," said Jenny. "She also mentioned a young man coming by once in a while, starting pretty recently."

"He doesn't sound neighborly," said Coutinho.

That was Jenny's impression. Otsaka's kind of isolation was a little unusual on this island. Family is huge in Hawaii, and most people his age would have had sons, daughters, nieces, nephews and vaguely defined hangers-on coming around at all hours.

"So we want an address book, photographs, anything that fills in the picture."

Jenny was the one who found the photo album in Otsaka's bedroom closet. Sammy kept rummaging in a dresser, as Coutinho took a seat at the kitchen table and started flipping through the book. When Jenny sidled up and studied the pictures over his shoulder, Coutinho didn't send her back to her task.

Langston Otsaka was one of those people who paste photos into an album without labels or context. He hadn't anticipated needing to help the cops solve his own murder, but it still frustrated them. Coutinho started at the back of the album and paged forward. The photos looked to be in rough chronological order, and the most recent ones might bear the most relevance to a violent death.

The first thing they saw was a a retirement party at a Hilo bar that Jenny recognized from the numerous fights she had broken up there. A date would have helped them check their files for a possible incident, but it couldn't be that easy. Otsaka himself looked at least ten years younger than the body on the morgue table.

"The county road crew," said Coutinho.

They knew Otsaka's employment history from his file, but Jenny also recognized some of the other men. She saw them at work on the roads, and she had pulled some of them out of pile-ups in this same bar.

Coutinho turned more pages. Otsaka kept getting younger, until he started appearing with a woman, an island mix of Portuguese, Japanese and Filipino. She looked younger than Otsaka, and as Coutinho flipped pages, she aged in reverse until she held an infant in her arms.

"Look at that face," said Coutinho. "I'm thinking motherhood wasn't exactly her dream job."

So what had happened to her? And where was the boy after his infancy? Could he be the young man the neighbors had seen?

"We need to find the wife," said Coutinho. "And the boy. He'd be, what, thirty-ish?"

"Probably."

"I'll ask at the high school."

Jenny liked the way he bounced that off her like a detective. But she was also ready when he sent her back on patrol. On her way out to 130 she passed a bright red RAV heading into the subdivision. Jack Holloway was behind the wheel. He didn't seem to notice her, although local residents knew what the blue cone on the roof of her Camry meant police.

He lived in North Hilo. Did he have a girlfriend out here in Pahoa? Jenny told herself that wasn't the only explanation for his presence, and she had no right to her twinge of jealousy.

The next day Coutinho intercepted her after roll call for the middle shift. She was on the way to her car. She reminded herself that mileage reimbursement forms were due.

"You're with me," he told her. "I cleared it with your sergeant."

"Where to?"

"We're going to canvas Otsaka's neighborhood again. We'll take your car."

Jenny's friend Kenny Lujan joined them in the parking lot. Coutinho seemed to see detective potential in him too.

She drove toward Pahoa through scrub brush that wasn't the first thing the Chamber of Commerce wanted visitors to see. Before they reached the town, Jenny turned left into the residential subdivisions. She parked in front of the Otsaka house, which had yellow crime scene tape across the front door.

"Ask the neighbors about the son," said Coutinho. "No Otsaka at Hilo High School for five years either side of 2007, which I thought would be roughly his graduation year."

"Check the other schools on the island?"

"We might have to, but I hope he turns up."

Jenny started knocking on doors. She soon learned from the neighbors that Otsaka's whitewashed box was the oldest on the street, and the other houses had sprung up around it.

"Nah," said Hez Kekua. "Never saw no young guy."

Hez for Hezekiah. Jenny had pulled him out of a bar fight or two, with some help, seeing as he was almost as big as Sammy Waga. Hez thought their history made them old friends. She could work with that.

"You find Langston's money yet?" he asked her.

"Money?"

"In his safe."

Jenny kept her poker face. The police had found no safe in Otsaka's house, but even if they had, they would have held the detail back from the public.

"Where'd he get this money?" she asked instead.

"He ran with some bad guys from Honolulu way back. They tried to muscle in on Morrison."

Anything to do with the biggest marijuana dealer on the island was above her pay grade, especially since a rookie police officer had met a presentable older man in a bar and spent the night with him.

He called himself Jim, as in Jim Morrison. Who else would a Sixties holdover and Vietnam veteran name himself after? Jenny suspected that Coutinho knew about her lapse, but they had never discussed it.

Now he might decide they had to deal with it. She found the detective in the back yard, looking into the lava tube as if he expected the goddess Pele to write the answer to everything on smoke and send it up to mortals on the surface.

"A safe," he said. "Terrific. That kind of urban folklore can stir up all kinds of craziness. I'll have to go ask Morrison about it."

He thought.

"Pakalolo. That's actually a relief, if it's not meth we're dealing with."

Jenny understood. The veterans of the marijuana industry, Morrison among them, liked things low-key. The new men of meth didn't have the same restraint.

"You can go back on patrol."

She tried not to look too relieved. Normally she would have been eager to tag along for the detective stuff, but keeping her distance from Morrison came first.

She reported in to Dispatch and got on the road.

• • •

Burglary in progress, in the same subdivision near Pahoa that had become Jenny's second home lately.

It meant responding without lights or siren. Every cop in the immediate vicinity would be running dark and feeling the same adrenaline rush. Burglars were usually local young men hustling pakalolo money. They seldom turned violent, but the difference between seldom and never could get somebody killed.

Jenny arrived ahead of anyone else. Coutinho had commented on her knack for being in the right place at the right time. She called it keeping her eyes and ears open.

It was only seven o'clock, but these semi-tropical islands made short work of twilight. One pass through the neighborhood reminded her of the layout, which told her what this call was about.

She parked several doors down from the address and got out. She had turned her Camry's courtesy off her first day on the job, and she wasn't sure it worked anymore.

Sammy appeared at her elbow. It always impressed her how quietly his three hundred pounds could move. More than one bad guy had mentioned it.

"Neighbor reported a moke or two sneaking around behind this house," he said in a voice that carried only as far as her ear.

"Which backs onto the Otsaka place," she said.

"Funny about that."

Kenny Lujan came up on the other side of Jenny.

"Dispatch says we're it," he said.

Four hundred Hawaii County officers on an island the size of Connecticut had to make do.

"Gotta make sure it isn't this house we want," said Sammy.

Jenny went up to the front door and looked it over, but the ambient light didn't do the job She covered most of the lens of her Maglight with her hand and played the reduced beam around the door. Nothing looked broken or disturbed.

She rejoined Kenny. After a few moments Sammy came around from the back.

"Looks okay. Let's do it."

They returned to their vehicles and drove around to the next street. They inspected the front door of Otsaka's house, which appeared intact. The crime scene tape was unbroken.

They walked around the house to the back yard. Right away Jenny saw a film of light fanning out on the fence that had saved her life. For a moment the illumination gave her a supernatural shiver. Light wasn't supposed to issue from the earth.

"Cover me," she told Sammy and Kenny.

It was kind of cool to get to say that, but she could have lived without the next part. She approached the man-eating hole and then got down to crawl.

The top of a ladder protruded about a foot from the ground. She could have used the help her first time here. Jenny braced her left hand on the ladder and played her flashlight downward with her right. A young man looked up at her from the bottom of the tube.

"Nate, what are you doing down there?"

She should have identified herself as a police officer, but the sight of her younger brother's childhood friend brought a less official response.

He froze for a moment and then looked around for inspiration. Nothing came.

"Howzit, Jenny?"

"No time for talk story, Nate."

He shrugged.

"Lookin' fo' get paid."

"Come on up out of there."

Nate climbed the ladder and planted his feet on the ground, which of course remained solid. Apparently the goddess Pele only wanted Jenny. The choice was Pele's prerogative, since she owned the islands.

Now three men looked at Jenny and waited for her next move.

"Okay, Nate, how are you gonna paid in a lava tube?"

"Everybody says the old man had lossa cash around. Wasn't in the house, or the cops woulda found it. Maybe it's down there."

"You didn't think we would look there too?"

"Well, if he hid it real good ..."

This urban legend was mutating at top speed. Maybe the cops should call the Sociology Department of the university for a way to squelch it.

"You see anyplace to hide money?"

"Not yet, but it's a big tube. Goes both ways."

Jenny recalled how Nate Cano had always operated on wishful thinking. Once again she thanked the Hawaiian gods for making her brother Ben recognize the dead end that this friend represented.

"Okay, Nate. Gotta take you in."

Cuffing him took seconds. Nate knew how it was done. Jenny kept a firm grip on Nate's elbow as she guided him around the house to her vehicle.

Headlights hit her face as she stowed Nate in her back seat. Somehow she knew who was behind the lights, even before Callen turned them off and climbed out of his Impala.

"It's handled," said Jenny.

"Just checking," said Callen.

"It's handled," said Sammy, looming out of the darkness.

Callen prudently said nothing as he returned to his car. Sammy had that effect on all the mokes, in uniform or out. Jenny sometimes envied his intimidation factor, although it could interfere with the rapport a detective needed to establish with suspects and witnesses.

An hour later she stood outside Interview Two with Coutinho and an assistant prosecutor named Rebecca Cordova. It didn't surprise Jenny to see the detective on a Tuesday night. Coutinho haunted the station from Monday through Wednesday, while his wife Lucy stayed in Honolulu working three twelve-hour days in the crime lab.

"This is a little embarrassing," said Cordova. "I'll have to look up the law on this one—whether the lava tube belonged to Mr. Otsaka. We might end up dealing down to trespassing. A confession to what the suspect was up to would help."

She addressed the last part to Coutinho, but he turned to Jenny.

"You'll get more out of him than anybody else."

Cordova didn't look happy about that. Jenny gave Coutinho points for ignoring the lawyer. She put her feet in motion before Cordova could think up an objection.

The sight of Nate looking so comfortable in jail depressed her, but Jenny shook the feeling off and read him the Miranda warning. He listened as if humoring her and signed the waiver.

"Whose idea was this?" she asked.

"Mine. Who else?"

He seemed proud.

"Where'd you come up with it?"

"I'm the idea man."

He still believed in himself, no matter how many times his notions led to nothing. Sometimes Jenny caught herself admiring his optimism.

"But this one, Caleb kinda got me thinking about it."

"Who's Caleb?"

"The old guy's son."

"He's here?"

"He was a few days ago."

"Where is he?"

"I ain't his mother."

"Okay, where was he a few days ago?"

Jenny reminded herself to take it one small step at a

time with Nate. He named the bar that she and Coutinho had just seen in Mr. Otsaka's retirement photos.

"Did you already know him?"

"Nah. He bought a round, and we wen' talk story."

"What did he talk about?"

"How he got sick of Vegas."

"What was he doing there?"

"Casinos. What else?"

There was a whole Hawaiian diaspora in Las Vegas. At some point an economic refugee from the islands had caught on in the casinos and hotels and brought his cousins and his cousins' friends to the Nevada desert, until now there must be a track worn into the ocean.

"But he came back."

"Yeah. Too hot there. Too much work."

Nate's tone said he empathized with a horror of work.

"What else did you talk about?"

"His father. How everybody thought he had money, but he didn't believe it."

"Did he tell you about the lava tube?"

"Yeah. Said the old man just showed it to him. It broke through a couple of years ago, while Caleb was in Vegas. His father never told anybody else about it."

"So why did he tell you?"

Nate fell silent as he thought about the question. It was just like him not to have considered it until this moment.

"I dunno."

"Think Caleb could have wanted you to get caught?"

"Why would he do that?"

Good question.

"Did he ever mention his mother?"

Now Nate looked totally confused.

"Never mind," said Jenny.

Coutinho met her in the hall.

"Sure wish he knew a little more."

"You get used to that with Nate," said Jenny.

"But we have Caleb Otsaka on the island."

He got busy with his phone.

3

"INTERESTING THAT THE LAVA TUBE didn't take Langston Otsaka by surprise," said Jenny. "That supports the homicide theory."

"Here's Caleb."

Coutinho showed her a standard LinkedIn profile and corporate portrait photo. Jenny studied it for a resemblance to the infant Langston's wife had held, but who looked like a baby picture?

"We can put a BOLO out," she said. "On him, and his mother too. Just in case."

"Done," Coutinho said.

"Oh. Right."

She tried to suppress her blush reflex, which of course dialed it up.

For three days the BOLO on Caleb or his mother

accomplished nothing. The airlines didn't ping them, and they didn't hitch a ride with any of the local companies running small plane or helicopter tours.

Then Dispatch sent Jenny to another street in Otsaka's subdivision.

"See the woman."

Jenny found the right whitewashed island box of a house and knocked. A woman opened.

"Mrs. Conyers?"

In spite of her name, the caller was a mostly Hawaiian woman in her fifties, and obviously old school in her billowing mu'u mu'u. Jenny felt her own body language adjust to the properly respectful posture.

"You real police or just playing?"

Jenny controlled her expression. What especially annoyed her was how often this reaction came from women. Ten or twenty years from now, age might give her some gravitas, but that didn't help now.

"I'm for real."

"Okay, then. Somebody messing with the old kine religion."

"Where's this, Auntie?"

"Come."

The woman closed her door behind her and started leading Jenny *makai,* downhill toward where the ocean met the sky like an enormous painting. The street dead-ended in scrub brush and tall grasses about Jenny's height.

Mrs. Conyers parted the grasses and revealed an informal trail worn into the red island dirt. They walked for three minutes and came upon a clearing. The woman pointed at four large flat stones scattered on top of the grass. The stones didn't belong to this landscape. A stream bed had worn them smooth long before someone gathered them and brought them here.

Adherents of the traditional Hawaiian religion used stones like these in their rituals. All over the island Jenny saw the stones stacked three or four high. But someone or something had knocked this shrine over.

The American Indian Religious Freedom Act extends to other indigenous groups, which made this vandalism a federal offense.

"Me, I'm a Baptist," said Mrs. Conyers. "But I see da old kine religion doing the young men some good."

She paused.

"I wouldn't mind if my son got involved with them."

Jenny couldn't think of anything helpful to say to that.

"Did this just happen?" she asked instead.

"Last couple of days. No idea who did it. Might be better all around if the police found them first."

Jenny started to walk around the clearing. It was something to do while she thought.

"Don't fall in," said Mrs. Conyers.

And of course it had to be another hole in the ground.

"That just opened up," she added. "Pele don't like ugly."

"Somebody should have told us," said Jenny.

"Telling you now."

Jenny was already tired of crawling on the ground, but

it had to be done. As she turned her flashlight on to peer into the hole, she felt maternal hands take her ankles.

"Careful there," said Mrs. Conyers.

Jenny blinked away the tears that came to her eyes. She had a mother, a very good one, but nobody's mother could be everywhere at once.

She put her mind on business and played her beam around the bottom of the hole. Mrs. Conyers must have felt Jenny tense, because she asked, "Not good?"

"Some people," said Jenny. "No damned respect."

She wondered where that had come from. Maybe Mrs. Conyers's hands on her ankles were transmitting traditional sentiments. Or maybe Jenny just didn't like people who trashed her island. Someone had eaten a KFC lunch down there and failed to police the area. She also saw a ladder lying flat on the bottom of the tube, which raised questions.

Was someone still down there?

She raised herself to her hands and knees. Mrs. Conyers released her ankles. Jenny took her radio from her belt and called Dispatch.

"I need backup and rescue to my location."

"Anything else?"

Jenny thought about that. Nate had mentioned that Otsaka's tube covered a lot of distance. This might be the same tube. She told the dispatcher the address of Langston Otskaka's place.

"Send a backup to stake out the skylight in the back yard. And notify Detective Coutinho."

• • •

As Jenny expected, Coutinho took one look and called out the Special Response Team, which led to more waiting. The men in black arrived in a departmental Ford Excursion. They grumbled as Fire Rescue lowered them into the tube.

"I'm betting it's the same tube," said Coutinho.

"That would make it a big one."

"We'll end up sending the rescue guys to the Otsaka place to haul the SRT's out again."

Almost an hour later his radio crackled. He listened and nodded in satisfaction.

"We called it."

He went to the fire crew and told them where to go. He returned to Jenny.

"I'm going to go out on a limb here," he said.

But then he waited for Jenny to say it.

"Somebody's looking for the money."

"Lot of commotion over money that doesn't exist."

"Unless it does."

• • •

"You've been busy, Nate."

He hadn't complained about being brought in again, but now he gave Jenny a suspicious look.

"What you mean?"

"You need to stay out of holes in the ground."

"Don't know what you're talking about."

She believed him. That was the thing about Nate. He couldn't pull off even the shortest con, because his face showed every thought that crossed his mind. Jenny probed and tried to confuse him with change-ups and curve-balls, but he stuck to his story.

She joined Coutinho in the hall.

"I don't see Nate messing with the religion. Good way to get his butt kicked, for one thing."

And even local non-believers would get a superstitious tingle at the idea of destroying a shrine.

"But," she said, "people who spent enough time on the mainland might lose the old attitudes."

"Vegas was on the mainland, last time I checked."

"We need to find Caleb."

That could be a problem. This huge island was a good place for hiding out, which could be done in two ways. Some legendary fugitives had lived off the grid in the rain-forest, but Caleb Otsaka probably hadn't picked up skills like that in the casinos.

The other way involved the Kona side of the island, where the vacation time-share jungle could hide a fugitive for months. But the BOLO was out, and finding anyone on the sunny side of the island was up to the cops of Kona Division.

Until Sergeant Silveira called her aside after roll call.

"Freitas. Got a once in a lifetime opportunity for you."

She waited.

"We're gonna lend you to Kona for three months."

"Kona? Why?"

"Don't let the sun get to you. It only feels like your hair is gonna catch fire."

Hilo natives like Jenny and the Sergeant shared a horror of the island's dry side. But the way he evaded her question gave Jenny a bad feeling.

"Inaba's going too. To hold your hand."

"Just let her try it."

But Patsy Inaba came from Kona originally. Jenny could expect some trash talk about the Hilo-Kona divide.

"What's this about?" Jenny tried again.

"The brass don't tell a sergeant."

She had her suspicions. This was about removing temptation, the temptation being Jenny. Patsy would come along to camouflage the purpose of the operation, never mind the effect on Hilo Division manpower. And the men who couldn't treat women as colleagues would end up looking like the victims.

Jenny swallowed her resentment. There was nothing concrete to point to, even if she wanted to start the grievance procedure.

She and Patsy both used their personal vehicles on patrol, which meant they had to drive separately around the island. Jenny preferred the southern route, which had her favorite ocean views and the best coffee stops. She and Patsy met up in Kona Division headquarters.

"Glad you didn't get lost," said Patsy.

"I thought about trying it, but who'd believe me?"

People called this "the easy island." It oversimplified things only a little to say there was one ring road around the whole island. Stay on the pavement and it was hard to go wrong, but the bad guys had a habit of taking to the mud roads around Hilo and moonscape dirt tracks of the Kona side.

So now the Kona Division had to find something for Jenny to do, and she hoped her assignment would keep her in the town of Kailua-Kona. She had been there before, and the learning curve would be shorter.

She also wouldn't mind getting the middle shift to start. It would help her ease into the new assignment, but right away her new sergeant put her on mornings. On her first day that meant dragging herself away from a poor night's sleep on a cot in the women's locker room and making breakfast out of bad station coffee and two donuts left over from the night shift.

Only cops could ruin coffee in Kona.

So she had two things to look for—real breakfast and a better place to crash.

"Freitas, Inaba, you're in Keauhou."

The next town to the south of Kona was ground zero for the condo explosion.

"Good news, girlfriend," Patsy told her on the way to their cars. "My uncle owns a two-bedroom right there, and he had a cancellation. Rent's a bargain for two, and the other bedroom is yours if you want it."

Kona and Keauhou also had restaurants. For a week Jenny tried one after another, but this side of the island got most of the visitors, and visitors minded these prices less than locals. It started to look as if Jenny was going to have to start scrambling eggs at five in the morning.

By the start of the second week she had resigned herself. She decided to enjoy one last breakfast out, and she chose Island Lava Java on Ali'i Drive, with one of the best views of Kailua Bay.

Most of the businesses in Kona employed college kids taking their summer break or a year off from school. The middle-aged woman behind the counter would have stood out a little under any conditions, but Jenny was already carrying a mental picture of Cindy Otsaka. The woman was older now, but Jenny had no doubt.

Since she usually changed into her uniform at the station, she was wearing civilian khakis and a white shirt draped open over a tank top. Looking like just another local young woman might help her get close to the woman.

But as she stepped up, Otsaka turned to the young man sharing counter duties with her. Her words got lost in the breakfast hubbub, but Jenny had no trouble reading her lips.

"Take over for a minute."

Otsaka's body language was too nonchalant as she made for the rear of the building. Jenny left the store by the front entrance and picked up her pace as she rounded the building. When the rear door opened, Jenny confronted the woman. She didn't bother to hold her shield up.

"We need to talk to you."

"I guess you do."

"Have we met?"

"I know a cop when I see one."

Jenny made a mental note to ask someone whether she had started looking like the job.

"Where's Caleb?" she asked.

"How would I know?"

"I'm going to detain you for questioning."

Jenny got her cell phone out and requested backup. Her cuffs were in the car. She settled for watching the woman's hands as she waited. Ten minutes later a middle-aged uniformed officer with the disheveled look of night shift cops everywhere rounded the corner of the building. His name tag said, "Alvares," in case he didn't already look Portuguese enough.

"Hey, new kid. Whatcha got?"

He looked at Cindy Otsaka, and his eyes widened.

"No shit. Good catch."

"I was just looking for breakfast, and there she was."

"Never ate here," he said. "Guess I should splurge once in a while. Okay, I'll take her in."

He gave her a fatherly look.

"You look hungry. Go."

4

THE DETECTIVE WAS a mostly Hawaiian man almost as big as Sammy Waga. Island ethnic mixing had given him the name Goldfarb.

"I just talked with Coutinho," he said.

His tone gave her an idea of what was coming.

"I thought he'd want to come out and question her, but he says give it to you."

Now he was looking her over in a way that usually meant a man was trying to imagine her naked. But he was searching her for detective chops, as if she wore them under her uniform. She found it refreshing, if also a little intimidating.

"You up for it?"

"Sure," she said before she could think about it too much.

An interview room was an interview room, always and everywhere. She took a seat across from Cindy Otsaka and studied her. Jenny liked the way the woman wore the road miles on her face, but Cindy's *tita* deadpan was less helpful.

"I think you've done this before," said Jenny.

"Sat down with the cops? A time or two."

"That's interesting, because you have no record."

"Try being married to Langston."

"What was he into?"

"You saw his file. Pakalolo."

Marijuana. The word took in a lot more than just growing a crop and selling it. Business disputes and general paranoia sometimes led to violence, despite Morrison's efforts to keep things calm.

"It's been a while, though. I got away from Langston ten years ago. I've been in Vegas too."

"So you must know what Caleb has been doing."

"We've got our own lives."

That sounded cold to Jenny, but maybe Cindy had learned her indifference the hard way.

"Would it surprise you to hear he's on the island?"

"He's got to be someplace."

"What would bring him here?"

"How would I know? Maybe his father's money. A lot of people believe that bullshit."

"So there was no money?"

"I never saw any."

"What brought you back?"

"I finally had to face it. I'm a Hilo girl. Vegas is too hot. People work too hard."

Jenny had heard that before, but it still wasn't adding up.

"Why did you run from me?"

"I guess I just fell into my old island kine habits. That's how I had to live with Langston."

Jenny probed and feinted, but she got nothing more.

"Can I go back to work now?"

"Sit tight for a minute."

She joined Goldfarb outside the room.

"I'd feel a lot better if we had Caleb to cross check stories," said Jenny.

"Go out and get lucky again."

She didn't take the comment as a dig. Jenny had heard Coutinho say more than once, "We'd rather be lucky than good."

"Cut her loose for now."

Goldfarb started back toward his office, but he turned and said, "Nothing wrong with making your own luck, though."

"I was thinking I might borrow Patsy."

He grinned.

"She's waiting for you in civvies. But I'm glad you thought of it."

Patsy's reputation must have accompanied her to Kona. She wasn't interested in detective stuff, but she loved the action on the street. Nobody beat Patsy with a rifle, but right now Jenny cared more about her friend's knack for tailing a suspect.

A team would have been better, but Hawaii County didn't have the manpower for an operation that might drag on and yield nothing.

While Patsy followed Cindy, Jenny went back on patrol and contended with one of the major differences between Kona and Hilo. Here rental cars covered every square inch of the town. Responding to a call involved finding a slot to wedge her car into. Her blue cone protected her from tickets or tow trucks, but even illegal spaces were hard to find.

She was doing a welfare check called in by yet another daughter in Vegas, whose mother wasn't answering the phone. Jenny dragged the mother out of bed, where she had spent the day with a boyfriend her daughter's age. Jenny was still grinning when her own cell phone sounded.

"I dunno, girlfriend," said Patsy. "She went straight back to her place. Hasn't moved in a couple of hours."

"The address she gave us?"

"Yeah. She's living like a college kid."

Many people in Hawaii lived four to a two-bedroom apartment, while working two jobs and a side gig to stay afloat.

"You seen any of the roommates?"

"Two young guys just left. The timing is right for restaurant dinner shifts."

Patsy snickered.

"Wonder if she's helping herself to any of that young stuff."

"There's a lot of that going on," said Jenny. "I don't suppose one of them was Caleb?"

"He'd be older than these guys."

"Hang on a little, anyway," she told Patsy. "See if anybody interesting shows up while she's there alone."

She drove some more, until her cell phone rang again.

"I had my sit down with Morrison," said Coutinho.

She listened to his report.

"Interesting. Guess I need to talk to Cindy again?"

At the last moment she remembered to make a question of it. The words had escaped before she considered them. It was up to Coutinho to decide whether she should continue with Cindy Otsaka, but he let her get away with her presumption.

"Do it," was all he said.

She called Patsy.

"Has she moved?"

"Nope. Are we going to go get her?"

Jenny told Patsy about her discussion with Coutinho.

"It would help if she made some motion," said Patsy. "Sarge said he needs me back on patrol soon."

"I'll swing by. Maybe if we both think good thoughts, she'll do something."

Only a quarter mile from Cindy's address a Malibu lurched out in front of Jenny. She could have pulled the car over for reckless driving, but instead she grabbed the legal parking space, which was even big enough to drive straight into instead of jockeying for five minutes.

Maybe she was getting her Kona chops. She found Patsy in a coffee place with a view.

"That's the place. Second floor, far right."

Someone had cloned the building from the hundreds of others in this town and dropped it where it would fit, although the land in Keauhou was disappearing fast. Jenny wondered whether local residents ever went to the wrong two stories and eight apartments, and how long they stayed before noticing their mistake.

The door opened, and Cindy Otsaka emerged carrying a knapsack.

"Good thoughts," said Jenny.

"Coutinho says you make things happen."

Jenny's face burned with embarrassment or pride or both.

"Drop me at my car."

"We'll lose her," said Patsy.

"I know where she's going."

Patsy gave her a skeptical look.

"Where?"

"Hilo."

Now Jenny wondered where her certainty had come from. But she thought about it, and it fit.

"Radio the sergeant. Have him call Coutinho. They'll work it out."

"You're sure about this?"

"Definitely. I want to beat her there."

They both climbed into Patsy's car in the coffee shop's tiny lot. Patsy drove to Jenny's Camry. If Jenny had been tailing Cindy Otsaka, she would have taken the blue cone off, but this time she wanted to stay ahead. She might need her flasher.

Coutinho would have Hilo Division officers stake her destination out, but Jenny wanted to get there in time for the action. She had just merged onto Highway 11, when her cell phone rang.

"She just left," said Patsy. "Red RAV. You sure about this?"

"I'm sure."

Five minutes later she got another call.

"You're en route?" Coutinho asked as if he knew the answer.

"I'll beat her there."

She hoped her bladder made it, because she couldn't afford the time for a stop. She had a pee bucket in the car, but it was for stakeouts, not high-speed contortions in the driver's seat. She kept checking her mirror in case Cindy Otsaka defied the reduced limits in the small towns that lined the southern route around the island.

Jenny passed from Kona sun into Hilo overcast. An hour later the brief subtropical twilight yielded to night.

Instead of continuing to Hilo, she turned right on 130 toward Puna. She went left into the subdivision where everything had started and decided she had a minute to use her bucket. In mid-pee her cell phone rang. She caught the call just before it went to voicemail.

"What's yours?" Coutinho asked.

"Two minutes away."

"We're inside. She won't be interested in the house."

She could have used the bathroom. Oh well.

Jenny's weeks in Kona had reminded her that the Hilo side of this island did darkness like few places in the nation.

She joined three other cops watching the shadow through the window slats in the rear of the darkened house. The men weren't much more than shadows themselves. The size of one of them could only mean Sammy Waga, and the bantamweight next to him had the body language of Kenny Lujan. Coutinho leaned closer to Jenny.

"Nothing down there."

"That's weird."

"I mean there wasn't, but there is now. We planted a duffel bag. Stuffed it with newspapers."

"Can't wait to see her face," said Jenny.

"We left the ladder. We'll let her go down and then take her."

Nothing would take the fight out of the suspect more effectively than looking up from the bottom of a lava tube at four cops who controlled the ladder.

Cindy Otsaka must have driven like a cowgirl. Twenty minutes before Jenny expected her, a form darker than the darkness slipped around the house and moved toward the back fence.

One moment the form was there, and the next it was gone.

"Go," said Coutinho.

She was already on her way out the back door, with

Kenny right behind her. Sammy's bulk made him lag a little, but he always made up for his lack of speed when he arrived.

Jenny looked around as she approached the fence, but everyone looked back at her. Wasn't it time for somebody else to deal with man-eating holes in the ground?

Apparently not.

"Somebody hold my feet," she said.

Kenny stepped behind her. She flopped down and crawled to the edge of the hole. Her flashlight was getting its exercise today. With Kenny holding her ankles, she played the beam downward and caught Cindy in the act of stepping off the ladder.

"Police," said Jenny. "Don't move."

As Cindy turned toward Jenny's voice, her left ankle nudged a large duffel bag. She ignored the item. That struck Jenny as J.D.L.R.

Just Doesn't Look Right—the instinct that every cop developed. Wasn't the bag what Cindy had come for?

"Come on up out of there," Jenny told her.

"You're getting to be a bad habit," said Cindy.

• • •

Coutinho's laptop showed Cindy sitting in Interview One and looking as self-contained as she had in Kona.

"You take her," said the detective.

Jenny expected the assignment, which made her feel better about the whole thing. Coutinho might give her the dirty work in lava tubes, but he also trusted her to question a suspect.

Three detectives were hanging around, watching and doing a poor job of hiding their disapproval. Coutinho ignored them.

He was counting on her to have built something of a rapport with the suspect, but now she had to prove him right. She took a minute to construct a bullshit file, padded with papers from the recycling bin, to give Cindy Otsaka the idea that the cops knew everything.

She opened the door. Cindy looked up at her. The woman's face still revealed nothing. Jenny took the seat opposite her.

"You're not under arrest. We're just talking. You can leave if you want."

A veteran of interactions with the cops might do that. Jenny tried to imply with her tone that her feelings would be hurt, and weren't they just girls in a boys' world?

"It was a pretty good idea," she said. "You figured the money would be in the place we had already searched. And you had Nate Cano telling the whole island there was nothing down in the tube. It was better than a safe."

Maybe Cindy would even spill who had put the money down there. But the woman didn't blink. Something still wasn't adding up.

"But I'm not under arrest?"

"Well, maybe the money is rightfully yours. You can help us establish that."

"If there's money, it's mine."

"Was it your husband's?"

"Must have been."

Cindy had just given herself a motive for murder, but Jenny refrained from pointing that out.

"So why were you working behind a counter? You must have known we would find you."

"I have nothing to hide."

"We're wondering who actually put the money there. You were on the other side of the island."

Cindy could have made an all-night round trip and gone to work, but somehow Jenny didn't think so.

The woman gave her more of her *tita* silence. Jenny decided on a diversion.

"We've been talking to Morrison."

Cindy blinked. That was a start.

"That's how he's stayed in business so long. He knows when to make himself useful."

"Why do I care?"

"I think you know. Morrison knew you way back, when Langston was running with the big boys from Honolulu. He told us a lot."

Not a flicker.

"He told us you were the brains of the outfit. Not everybody knew that, but Morrison knows what he needs to know. So guess what else he told us."

Jenny leaned in.

"He told us you didn't raise Caleb."

"Bitch."

Jenny gave the woman a little space and softened her tone.

"Postpartum depression is the bitch. I'm not a mother, but obviously I have one. I know some mothers who have had it. I know it's a terrible thing. Morrison told us Langston came to him. Even thirty years ago Morrison was running Puna. Keeping everything low key so the cops didn't have to get involved."

It raised questions about what Jenny had been doing when she spent the night with Morrison, but Cindy didn't need to know about that. Neither did the detectives listening in. Morrison wouldn't tell as long as it was in his interest to keep their secret.

"Langston told him he was desperate. He couldn't leave you alone with the baby. He had to get Caleb away from you more than once. Morrison took Caleb and gave him to an ex-girlfriend."

Trust Morrison to keep his exes on the kind of terms that made them useful. Jenny wondered when he would come to her about something.

"She was going to Vegas, and she took Caleb. Did you know that part, or did Caleb just disappear?"

"I knew. She was welcome to him."

"Because he'd have a better chance at life."

"Because I didn't want him. I wasn't depressed."

Jenny considered the woman across from her. Cindy might be in denial, or she might just be a bad mother. In just three years on the job Jenny had seen more than enough of the phenomenon. Sometimes the relevant genes got deleted from the double helix, or the motherhood synapses just didn't fire.

"Being pregnant wasn't bad. Compared to what some women say, I had it easy. I wouldn't have minded doing the surrogate thing to get paid for it. What the hell."

Cindy sat and remembered.

"But he was the ugliest thing I ever saw. And Jesus, the noise, and the smell."

"So let's fast-forward thirty years. How did you connect with him in Vegas?"

"He came looking for me."

"How did he know where to look?"

"No idea."

"You didn't ask?"

"I assume you want to make detective. In that case you need to be a better listener. I didn't care enough to ask. I thought that was obvious."

"Okay, whose idea was getting close to Langston?"

"I don't know. It just came up. Caleb wanted to talk, and what did we have to talk about except Langston? And this money he supposedly had."

"What was the plan?"

"Worm our way back into his life, what else? Langston bought it. What a pathetic old man he turned into."

"So who hit him?"

"No idea."

"Caleb?"

"Maybe. He's stupid enough. If there was money,

nobody had to kill Langston for it. We just had to take it and go. Who was he going to complain to about it?"

Cindy's face closed down.

"I'm talking too much. Am I under arrest?"

"Well, there's trespassing. But we're not going to make an issue of it."

Without another word Cindy got up. Jenny walked her to the exit in silence and watched the woman use her cell phone. Ten minutes later a Ford Escape turned into the station. Jenny knew the driver. Lanny Soares supplemented his meager earnings as one of the island's few private investigators by driving for Uber.

She went back inside and found Coutinho.

5

"*DID MORRISON TELL* us everything he knows?" Jenny asked.

"Morrison never tells anybody everything," said Coutinho.

"Maybe I should ask him."

Damn. Jenny hadn't seen that coming. Coutinho fixed her with his detective look, the one he aimed at suspects when warmth and understanding failed to get results. This time there was nobody around to absorb it but her.

"Sure you want to do that?"

"Not at all. But I'll try it if it might get us something."

"It's awkward," said Coutinho. "We'll have to clear it with the drug guys. They might be sitting on Morrison."

Who would then want to know why Coutinho had chosen a uniformed officer, little more than a rookie, to send into the devil's den. And the drug guys knew Morrison's weakness for young women.

Jenny wasn't sure it was a weakness. He held the upper hand with her if he ever chose to use it.

"That's if I go to his house for a sit down," she said. "But suppose I ran into him someplace. Like Luquin's?"

Now she was really pushing it. The bar of the Mexican restaurant at the heart of Pahoa's nightlife was where her near-downfall with Morrison had started.

"We know he hangs there," said Coutinho, "and I'd be able to keep an eye."

She took his comment to mean that his confidential informant on the restaurant staff would be watching. She still didn't know the informant's identity.

Coutinho made her meet his eyes once more before he said, "Okay, let's do it."

That night Jenny dressed the way she remembered going to Luquin's on the night she met the silver fox whose name hadn't seemed to matter at the time.

Tonight he occupied the same stool.

"Officer," he said without turning his head.

Jenny wasn't the only woman on the island who wore khaki shorts, sandals and a blue chambray shirt. She could see a couple of similar outfits right here in the bar. But Morrison hadn't survived more than thirty years in his illegal business without learning to anticipate the cops.

"Mr. Morrison."

Immediately she felt down a point. She had never

settled on what to call him, and the honorific sounded a little weird applied to a man she had seen naked.

"Just Morrison is fine," he said. "What can I do for the Hawaii County Police?"

"I'm here to pick your brain."

"Just my brain?"

She let him get away with that one.

"We're having trouble filling in Caleb Otsaka's resume."

"It's interesting, isn't it?"

"I don't suppose he ever wrote you a thank you note? You may have saved his life."

"I doubt Valerie ever told him my part."

"Valerie who?"

"Spencer at the time."

"And now?"

"She married a guy named Calatrava. Do the math."

"Italian plus Vegas," said Jenny.

"I assume they're still together. It's hard to divorce the mob."

That was interesting, although Jenny wasn't sure why. But none of this was information that Coutinho couldn't have obtained from Morrison. She needed to do better.

"I'm impressed with how you handle your exes."

"Some of them would object to the concept of being handled. And I would expect you to be one of them."

Jenny decided two digs were enough. Three, and she would dig back. But right now business called.

"Sounds as if Mr. Calatrava didn't adopt Valerie's son."

"He didn't need to. She gave him two sons of his own."

Morrison drank from his bottle of Negro Modelo.

"Ever seen *The Godfather?*" he asked.

"I read the book."

For the first time he looked at her.

"No kidding. I didn't think your generation read anything but Twitter."

There was that third dig.

"Maybe you're losing touch. It might be time to move up to someone more age appropriate."

"Ouch," he said without heat. "So you know about Tom, right? The adopted son who accepted his role as a loyal consigliere. Maybe Caleb went that route. Or maybe being adopted gave him major attitude."

"Like he had something to prove."

"And he thought coming back to Vegas with a big score would do it."

"Maybe you can help me find out."

"Why would I want to do that?"

"Old times?"

"One night hardly qualifies."

"Then I've got nothing."

He gave her a steady look, and the effort it took to return it impressed her. In another lifetime he might make a good detective.

Morrison broke off the contest and took out a cell phone. When he selected a number from his contacts, he impressed her again. She kept things pleasant with her exes when she encountered them, but she didn't go as far as storing their numbers.

Jack Holloway came to mind, which struck her as a little strange. As exes went, the EMT had less seniority than some other young men on the island.

Morrison didn't need to identify himself. Valerie must have kept his number as well. They got right down to business. Morrison asked about Caleb, which led to several minutes of listening. He thanked her and disconnected.

"You're going to find this interesting. Valerie hasn't seen him in over a year. And Caleb might not be Caleb anymore."

Jenny's mind skipped several steps.

"WITSEC?"

"For a while. She heard he bailed out of the program, though."

"What did he do to get admitted in the first place?"

"Testified against his stepfather. Who then beat the charges."

To Jenny it sounded as if Caleb had turned against his whole life in Nevada, which might have given him the idea of reconnecting with his roots. But that hadn't gone well either.

"You know what else I read about?" she said. "Lee Harvey Oswald. Bouncing back and forth between America and Russia, falling in and out of love and never settling on either one."

"I won't underestimate you again," said Morrison.

Which told her he was following her line of thought. Coming home to Hawaii wasn't working out any better for Caleb than the life WITSEC had given him. Anything could happen now, and cops hated unpredictability.

"Thanks," she said as she slid off her stool.

"I'd say anytime, but it wouldn't be true."

She decided to let him have that one. It would cover her escape.

Coutinho grasped the problem too.

"So now we have to keep our eyes open for wise guys on our territory. And they won't be here for a vacation."

"I don't suppose they'd just let it go," said Jenny.

Instead of replying, he took his cell phone out and made a call, which was all listening on his end. He disconnected.

"I asked Kona Division to keep an eye. They just went around to Island Lava Java. Cindy didn't show up for work."

He looked around the bullpen.

"Any guesses about where she went?"

He was fair about it. He didn't fix his eyes on Jenny, but he was asking her. She was the one who supposedly had the rapport with their suspect.

But she didn't have an answer, and neither did anyone else.

"Better get back to Kona," said Coutinho, and this time he did address her. "I'll tell your sergeant you're coming."

So he would know when to expect her. No nap for Jenny.

By Monday morning Jenny had caught up a little on her sleep. She was an hour into the morning shift, when dispatch sent her to coffee country south of Kona. The address turned out to be a bean distributor's warehouse near the hamlet of Captain Cook.

"Mr. Hanson?"

Longtime residents of European descent got to looking as if someone had left them out in the sun for fifty years. They lost every ounce of body fat and took on the color of a high-end leather attaché case.

"Thanks for coming out, Officer. I opened up after the weekend, and I found something you should see."

He started walking her deeper into the warehouse, and Jenny got a feeling about what he wanted to show her. The feeling came from the height of the warehouse. Life on this island was a ground floor affair. There were few basements and even fewer second stories.

But this case had started with a deadly fall, and the warehouse had the vertical room for another one.

The feeling got worse when Hanson showed her a stain on the floor. Fluorescent lights high overhead gave everything an unnatural tinge, but Jenny knew blood when she saw it. The amount might or not be survivable. Someone had done some ineffectual mopping up, but the outline remained. She looked around. Heavy-duty shelves along the rear wall reached to the ceiling.

"I got my ladder and looked. Somebody's been camping out up there. Sleeping bag, beef jerky, packs of raisins and stuff. I just left it."

"How'd they get in?"

"Well, nobody broke in, and I always look around before I lock up."

To Jenny that sounded like an inside job She got her cell phone out.

•••

Goldfarb was the first detective on the scene. The crime scene people from Kona Divison arrived right behind him.

"This might bear on the Otsaka case," said Jenny.

That was stretching it. She had nothing but a feeling, but a detective like Goldfarb knew about hunches.

"Call him."

Coutinho showed up around noon and checked with Goldfarb. Parts of the discussion drifted to Jenny as she guarded the scene, in case the workers strayed too close. Goldfarb had told Hanson he could go about his business in the front part of the warehouse.

"She's lucky," said Coutinho. "Stuff happens when she's around."

"Luck beats smarts," said Goldfarb.

"Which she also has."

Jenny tried to keep her professional poker face, but a smile broke through. She turned away so they wouldn't catch her. When she turned back, Coutinho was standing right in front of her.

"No proof it's Caleb hiding out here," he said.

"There's the man cave aspect of it," she said. "It's definitely a young guy."

"No shortage of those."

Without a body, the crime scene work went faster than Jenny had expected. She still had a lot to learn about this stuff. Goldfarb sent her back on patrol with an hour left on her shift.

At least she didn't have to be Hanson. She left the man frowning over the bloodstain and wondering how to make it disappear.

•••

"Found her," said Coutinho.

"Cindy? What's she saying?"

"Not much. She's dead."

Not what Jenny had been expecting to hear.

"Where did she turn up?"

"Pu'u O'o. Laid out for the taking, but nothing doing."

Jenny followed his train of thought. Pu'u O'o was ground zero for the thirty-year eruption, but sometimes the lava slowed to inches an hour for no reason that mortal humans could discern. Whoever had given Cindy to Pele must have forgotten that the goddess sometimes spurned offerings.

Which suggested someone who had been off the island a long time

"A couple of hikers found her. What would we do without them?"

Visitors who explored the island beyond the beaches often served as the eyes and ears of the overextended police department.

"What's Dr. Ramesh say?"

"Nothing yet. Get back here for the autopsy."

By now she knew not to ask if he had cleared it.

• • •

"Injuries all in one plane," said Dr. Ramesh. "Except."

He leaned over the body to examine a depressed fracture in the back of the head.

"Where have we seen that before?"

Jenny didn't bother to reply. Everyone remembered Langston Otsaka's autopsy.

"Does getting hit on the head run in this family?"

Coutinho didn't encourage levity at the expense of victims of violence, but this was Dr. Ramesh's territory, and he tended toward grim M.E. humor. Coutinho ignored the question and offered one of his own.

"So is this the body that goes with the blood in the warehouse? I guess we'll have to wait on the lab results."

Coutinho started toward the door. Jenny followed him down the hall until the odors of death petered out. He stopped and turned toward her.

"How do you see it?"

"It still looks like a man cave on that shelf."

Coutinho grinned.

"You've seen a few of those?"

"My *fadda* has one. And I have been known to go out on the occasional date."

She refrained from asking him whether he maintained a man cave of his own, but Lucy Coutinho was smart enough to allow one such room on her premises.

"I think Caleb's been hiding out there, and Cindy knew it. Maybe she even found the place for him and set it up."

Coutinho nodded at that.

"I've been wondering how they got in without breaking anything. You're thinking ..."

"Cindy knows how to manipulate young guys. I think we should look at the workers at that place."

"Okay," he said. "Get back to Kona. I'll find you there."

Which he did before eight the next morning. He must have been on the road well before dawn. Hanson didn't look pleased to see them.

"We need to talk to your workers," said Coutinho. "We'll try to keep the disruption to a minimum, but this is a murder case now."

"I get it," said the boss.

He retreated to his office.

Jenny looked around. A half dozen men were lifting and hauling burlap bags. Three were middle-aged men who could have traded places with Hanson with hardly anyone noticing—maybe not even their wives.

The other three were closer to her age. One would resemble the older men in twenty years, but that was then. Now his blond surfer looks were the kind that turned her head.

Off duty, of course. He challenged her with a look, and a cop couldn't back down, could she?

Honor satisfied, she evaluated the other two. Neither quickened her pulse. One was pudgy and pale enough to have arrived in Kona yesterday. The other was so scrawny that he didn't look equal to hefting fifty pound bags of coffee beans, but breaking up bar fights had taught Jenny that men with his type of build could surprise her with their strength.

"So," said Coutinho "Who looks like he's been getting some recently?"

Jenny caught herself before she gave him a look of surprise. That was tame for the average cop, but almost crude coming from Coutinho.

"And can't believe his luck," she said.

She evaluated the surfer again. He was likely to have experience with cougars from the mainland. Jenny decided that Cindy have passed over him in favor of someone easier to manipulate.

She nodded at the pale young man. He looked away and seemed about to panic and run.

"Him."

"Go get him," said Coutinho.

6

JENNY MARCHED UP to the young man.

"What's your name?"

His voice took three tries before it worked.

"Dave James."

Was it the uniform or the attractive young female factor that was making him nervous?

Both, probably.

"I have some questions for you."

She knocked on the office door and opened it. Behind his desk Hanson looked up, even less pleased.

"Can we borrow your office, Mr. Hanson?"

He got up and left carrying his laptop. Jenny suppressed a grimace. Too often, a cooperative citizen paid a price in inconvenience. That citizen might talk to other citizens and make them reluctant to help the police. She took his seat behind the desk and let Dave James stand in front of her for a moment like a schoolboy.

"Sit."

He complied, and she stared at him some more.

"So how did you meet her?"

"Who?"

"Too late for that, Dave. I'm talking about the hot older babe."

He wore a mulish look on his face. She called up a photo of Cindy on her phone.

"Her."

"Bar," he said.

It was going to be one of those interviews. She would have to pry his story out of him one word at a time.

"How did it happen?"

"She came on to me. I swear."

"What was her name?"

"Jennifer."

Jenny tried not to react. Apparently she had made an impression on Cindy.

"Okay, you met her in the bar."

"And we're talking, and I'm thinking she's going to see somebody she likes better and drop me."

His tone said it had happened before.

"But then she says, 'Let's get out of here.' I couldn't believe it."

"Where do you live?"

"*Mauka.*"

As if she wouldn't know the pidgin term, he pointed uphill.

"With *ohana?*"

"Yeah. My mom would probably notice if I brought somebody home."

"But you knew how to get in here after hours."

He hesitated. Jenny didn't tell him the boss had already figured it out. Hanson trusted people, but he had a brain.

"I know where the spare key is. Everybody here does."

"So you brought Jennifer here and got busy."

"Yeah."

"And she sprang it on you that she needed a place to hide out for a while."

"Yeah."

She kept the pressure on with her eyes.

"I told her she had to be out by six every morning. And she was."

"Sit tight."

Jenny got up and went to find Coutinho. He was looking up at the shelves where the overnight guest had hidden. She filled him in.

"I can't see Cindy staying here," she said. "I think she was stashing Caleb."

"That's my take," he said. "But it's getting complicated. I just got a call from the lab. The stain is Cindy's."

"So who knocked her off the shelf?"

For the next several days the question intruded at odd moments, as she patrolled and took reports of burglaries in condos and hotel rooms. Sometimes she wondered when mainland visitors would decide that these islands weren't worth the trouble.

Then Dispatch sent her and Patsy down the coast, almost to Kaena, the southern tip of the island. The man they were supposed to find had warrants, and Goldfarb's CI said he was sleeping rough. They signed out a departmental Ford Escape to handle the off-roading to a known homeless encampment on a remote beach. The vehicle bounced Jenny without mercy, and the sun drilled through her sunglasses.

"Should we split up?" Patsy asked.

"I'm thinking no. We're our own backup on this."

Help was hours away at the speeds even four-wheel drive could manage on this terrain.

They went among the tents, calling into each one. There were no doors to knock on, but court decisions had given the residents of the camp an expectation of privacy.

In the end they accomplished nothing except drying their skin out in the relentless sun and wind. Either their man was away, maybe at a job, or the CI had it wrong to begin with.

But on their way back to the Escape they met a different man coming the other way.

"We've been looking for you," said Jenny.

"Guess you found me," said Caleb Otsaka.

"We have some questions for you."

He shrugged. Jenny suppressed a sense of anticlimax, as she and Patsy walked him to their vehicle and stowed him in the front passenger seat. As a witness he didn't get the cuffs, but Patsy sat behind him in case he acted up. He withdrew into his own thoughts and barely reacted to the merciless pummeling that the terrain inflicted on the way back to the highway.

Jenny had seen it before. The stress and exhaustion of trying to live off the grid often made a fugitive want to get caught.

Back in the Kona station Patsy escorted Caleb to an interview room. Goldfarb joined Jenny in watching Caleb on the laptop screen.

"Is Coutinho coming back?" she asked him.

"He says let you take it."

Jenny found herself wishing Goldfarb would give her a hint what he thought about that, but a detective never let anyone read his mind.

"Okay."

• • •

"Vegas," said Jenny. "You're a pretty rare bird."

"What's that mean?"

"Lots of *kama'aina* in Vegas. Most of them dreaming about coming home. You did it."

"I could have done it better."

"What are you calling yourself these days?"

"You know about that?"

"That you were in WITSEC? Yeah, We don't have any details."

"I'm Caleb Otsaka. Anybody wants me, come and get me."

That didn't square with hiding in a homeless encampment, or a warehouse, but there could be other reasons for that.

"Was it harder to get by without your … ?"

Jenny wasn't sure what to call Cindy. Did Caleb even know she was his mother?

"I don't know what to call her either. I only have her word for it that she's my mother."

"How did you connect with her?"

"She found me in Vegas. Said she'd been looking for me."

That already contradicted Cindy's account.

"Why did she want you?"

"She wanted help ripping off my father. What else?"

"And you were okay with that?"

"He was nothing to me. I didn't even know him."

"So this woman shows up out of nowhere and says she's your mother."

"She had pictures of her and an infant. Definitely her. Me, who knows?"

That didn't jibe with Cindy's indifference to her husband and son. Had she saved up blackmail material for decades? That would be cold.

"So she tells you your father has all this money, and you just say, sure, let's do it?"

"Well, no. She had to convince me the money was real."

"How did she do that?"

"She said she'd show me."

"How?"

"Well, we had to come to the island, obviously."

"And you just dropped everything and went."

"Well, I was kind of at loose ends."

"That's an understatement."

"If you already know, why are you asking me?"

"We always want to get your side of the story."

"Okay, yeah, I had to get out of Vegas. And witness protection wasn't for me. They wanted to send me to fucking Alaska. I hate winter."

"So your mother told you about this money and you went."

"Yeah."

"And she introduced you to your father?"

"No, she didn't go near him."

"Why not?"

"She said it would make him suspicious. So I went up and knocked on the door."

"How did he react to that?"

"It was pathetic. Like I was the prodigal son or something."

"Weren't you?"

"I played along. It wasn't hard, because his mind was going. Sometimes he would call me Caleb and sometimes I was Abel."

Caleb, Cain. Close enough for a confused mind, and these devout islands marinated in Bible lore.

"So you played along to get the money."

"Easiest gig I ever had. He couldn't wait to show it to me. Said it was mine when he was gone."

"So you decided to speed things up."

"What? No. I was just going to take it."

"You were going to?"

"He moved it. One day the safe was there, and the next day it wasn't."

The famous safe had been real.

"I guess he wasn't as pathetic as you thought. Or your mother."

"Yeah. She was pissed."

"What was she doing all this time?"

"Just hanging out. With that friend of hers. Mrs. Conyers."

Jenny blinked. She remembered maternal hands on her ankles as she peered into the earth, and she couldn't square that with Cindy Otsaka's murderous plans. Cindy must have been exploiting the woman the way she did everyone else.

Then Jenny recalled something else Mrs. Conyers had said. She filed it away to run it by Coutinho.

"Who killed your father?"

"No idea. I sure didn't."

"Did your mother?"

"I told you, I don't know. I don't think so."

"What happened in the warehouse?"

"What warehouse?"

"Where you've been hiding out."

"You know where I've been hiding out. You just found me there."

One grim hideout was probably enough. But Jenny studied him and wondered how to verify his claim.

"Sit tight," she said.

Goldfarb met her out in the hall.

"You're supposed to narrow the suspects down, not add more."

She saw a flash of humor behind his deadpan. At least, she hoped that was what it was.

7

THE DRIVE AROUND the island was starting to feel like her morning commute, just hours long. Coutinho met her as she entered the station on Kapiolani Street. He sent her to his office and joined her there a minute later. He placed a cup of coffee in front of her on his partner's desk. No milk, no sugar, when she would have preferred both, but if that was how detectives took it, she would learn to like it. He listened to her report.

"Remember Mrs. Conyers?" she asked him. "Cindy was spending time with her."

"Do we think she was involved in this?"

"I think Cindy had her fooled."

Coutinho typed into his laptop and studied the results for a while. He turned the screen toward her.

"What I was thinking," she said.

He got up.

"Let's go talk to her."

Jenny chugged the rest of her coffee and followed him out. He drove his personal Camry toward Pahoa and turned into the homelands estates.

Mrs. Conyers opened her front door.

"Officer Freitas. And Detective Coutinho. You're here about my son. Come in."

Jenny expected to end up in the kitchen, and Mrs. Conyers didn't disappoint her. On the way they passed through meticulously kept rooms of furniture that must have come from the woman's own grandmother. The kitchen smelled of shoyu and five-spice seasoning.

All the marks of a good auntie.

Mrs. Conyers pointed at the kitchen table. Coutinho waited for the hostess to sit and took the chair across from her. As the youngest in the room, Jenny was the last to sit.

"So, what did Kimo do?"

Under the matter-of-fact tone lurked deep sadness. Jenny wanted to put a hand on the woman's arm, but professional detachment prohibited sympathetic gestures.

"Nothing we know of," said Coutinho. "But he might know something about Langston Otsaka. Where is Kimo now?"

"You find out, let me know. Haven't seen him in quite a while."

Jenny had seen that hard-earned indifference on the faces of many parents.

"How about Cindy Otsaka? We hear she's been around."

"She was for a while, but that was weeks ago."

"You and Cindy were friends?"

"Neighbors. A neighbor comes for help, you help."

"She needed a place to stay?"

"That's what she said. All of a sudden I'm thinking 'hide out' would be more like it."

"Did Cindy and Kimo meet?"

"They did."

"How did they get along?"

"Like something was going on between them, and they didn't want me to catch on."

"What kind of something?"

"Probably something that involved money but not work. That's always Kimo's style."

"How about anything sexual?"

Mrs. Conyers was the kind of woman who always sat with a straight back. But somehow outrage found a way to lengthen her spine even more.

"She's old enough to be his mother."

The spine began to wilt, and she spoke in a lower voice.

"Kimo's my youngest. He came along almost ten years after the others, when I thought I was done with all that."

The two cops waited.

"What I'm saying—Cindy could be his mother, but I think a lot of young men wouldn't mind that. But if she got involved with a young man, it wouldn't be for fun. There would have to be something in it for her."

"Cindy's dead," said Coutinho. "Somebody killed her."

He let Mrs. Conyers take that in. Jenny found her stoic front impossible to read.

"So you see why we need to talk to Kimo. Maybe he didn't have anything to do with it, but we need to find out."

"He's my son."

"He'll always be your son," said Jenny. "No matter what."

"I'll do what I can."

Outside by the car Coutinho stopped and aimed a look at her, until she wondered what was coming.

"Nice moves, Officer."

"Wish it felt better."

"Wish I could tell you it will after a while. But that's when you should worry."

He gave her a slight smile.

"Here endeth the detective lesson for today. Call in to Sergeant Silveira."

"I'm in Kona."

"Not anymore. The Chief said, what the hell. If I'm going to keep bringing you back here, you might as well stay."

"There's a problem here that hasn't gone away."

"We're working on it."

• • •

The bar felt like home.

Jenny sat in her car in the parking lot and waited for word to filter into the place and reach Nate. He emerged more or less on schedule, but he was stumbling and holding his nose as blood seeped between his fingers.

That wasn't all. Two more young men came running out after him and kept going. Jenny knew them both. When they moved that fast, there was a fight going on that they wanted no part of.

Or someone had offered them a job.

She didn't have time for this, but as the cop on the scene, she owned the situation. First thing, backup. She got on the radio.

They came within three minutes. She had to give them that much. But the aging white Impala and the dark blue Malibu belonged to Callen and his friend Dumas.

The sight of Jenny gave them no pleasure, either. Someone had been talking to them about her. They met by the entrance to the bar.

"We're it," said Callen. "Might as well do it."

Jenny checked her taser and took her baton from her belt. When she looked up, the two young men were waiting for her to go first.

Okay, somebody had to. She pushed through the door and walked into a wall of heat and hormones from the kind of exertions that had been culling the male herd for thousands of years. Jenny felt the usual impulse to let them do what came naturally, but the citizens of Hawaii County didn't pay her to look the other way.

The main action was a knot of half a dozen men in the middle of the floor. If they ran out of fight, the peripheral battles would stop on their own.

A Hawaiian man in a tank top and board shorts was letting loose a barrage of shots to the midsection of a tall, lean *haole,* while another man held the victim. Jenny snapped her baton open and rapped the big man on the knob of his elbow. He stopped throwing punches, but that was due more to surprise than pain. He turned and threw his other fist at her. She blocked it with the baton, but the impact sent her airborne. She landed on her feet, but that kind of luck wouldn't continue. She spared a tenth of a second on glancing behind her.

Her two colleagues were standing against the wall and watching. Did they plan to post an online review?

She turned back and nearly walked into a punch. She ducked just enough for the huge fist to graze the top of her head. Even that was a wallop. This was getting bad.

A bar stool appeared above her opponent. The stool came down hard on the big man's head. He staggered and sat heavily on the floor.

Now Jenny could see her rescuer, another Hawaiian man dressed in the same local uniform. She had never met him, but she had been looking at his mugshots.

"Kimo," she said. "Been wanting to talk to you."

● ● ●

"I used up a lot of luck there," said Jenny.

Coutinho's face said he understood. In the academy and on the street, cops absorbed the lesson—never count on the assistance of civilians. Jenny was walking upright because a civilian had stepped up while Callen and Dumas acted like civilians. Should she make an issue of it?

The decision would have to wait, because now she had to treat Kimo as a suspect.

"This time it's a no-brainer," said Coutinho. "You talk to him."

Even Cordova nodded in agreement.

• • •

"Thanks," said Jenny. "That was getting bad."

"I owed him one anyway."

"You guys were feuding?"

"Pakalolo stuff. You know da kine. What happened with your backup?"

Jenny couldn't discuss the issue with someone outside the department. But if Coutinho, watching on his laptop, caught on to Kimo's implication, could anyone blame her?

"They were busy."

The words tasted bad to her. Was she really going to be just another woman defending men for the indefensible?

"What I need to ask you about—your mother had a friend staying with her for a while."

"She get a lot of friends. Which one?"

"I think you remember this one."

She showed him one of the old photos from Langston Otsaka's album, scanned into the computer system.

"Cindy," he said.

Cindy had used her real name this time, because Mrs.

Conyers already knew her. Jenny gave him a conspiratorial smile.

"She still looks good, doesn't she?"

He gave her an uncomfortable shrug.

"So where have you been lately."

"Business."

"With Cindy?"

"What kine business I got with a friend of my mother?"

"Okay, maybe it wasn't business."

She put some girl-boy mischief into her tone, and his moke façade slipped for a moment, revealing a boyish smile. It was as good as a confession, and he must have realized it, because he put his tough guy deadpan back on. But now it was definitely an act.

"So where did you go with her? I doubt your mother would put up with that stuff in her house."

"We went down in the lava tube."

"She was okay with that?"

Jenny remembered some pretty grim settings for furtive experiments with teenage sex, and college hookups had often taken place on dorm beds that had room for two bodies only if they were stacked one on top of the other. But at the bottom of a lava tube? She wouldn't have put up with that at sixteen, let alone at Cindy's age.

"Okay, so you're down in the tube with Cindy. Whose idea was it to get it on down there?"

"Hers."

"Tell me about the first time."

"Why? You into that stuff?"

"Maybe I want some pointers. She keeps the young kine guys interested."

This discussion was making Jenny feel grimy. She hoped it yielded something soon.

"She wanted to explore the place."

"Did she say why?"

"She said it might connect with her property. Hers now her old man was dead."

"Why with you?"

"I used to go down there a lot. Just for something to do."

"Used to?"

"Kid stuff."

"But Cindy got you interested again."

"Well, she was into it."

"Okay, so you're exploring."

"And she was really pushing it. Lots farther than I ever went. Then this one time, all of a sudden she shuts off her flashlight, and she's all over me."

"She liked it in the dark."

"But there's dark, and then there's dark. Down there, that was too much dark for me."

Jenny sat back and evaluated him and his clueless expression. He didn't seem to be thinking what she was thinking.

What had Cindy seen that she didn't want him to notice?

"What opening did you use to get in?"

"The new one. By the stones."

"You remember where you went from there?"

"I think so. Probably the farthest I ever went down there."

"I want you to show me."

"You're gonna ruin my reputation, Officer. I mean, I don't mind helping you out in a fight, but ..."

"You don't need points with the cops?"

"Don't want to get caught earning them."

"I don't mind if you talk story a little. You know da kine."

Using the Cindy Otsaka playbook made her feel even more soiled, but whatever worked. Coutinho would understand, but Rebecca Cordova wasn't a cop. She just used the good stuff that the cops brought her without getting her own hands dirty.

Like every other civilian.

• • •

Coutinho wasn't happy.

Kimo was refusing to go underground with anyone but Jenny. He wasn't facing charges, which took their leverage away. He could just say no.

"I'll let you go first, just you and Kimo, but then I'm sending the SRT's after you. Not negotiable."

"They'll have to stay back," said Jenny.

"Understood."

She could see she had some fences to mend with him after maneuvering him into this operation.

"I still don't like it," he said. "Communications will be hit or miss down there."

"No choice," said Lieutenant Tanaka.

Jenny had never seen the lieutenant's office from a detective's perspective before. She squelched the smile that threatened to break out at an inappropriate moment. She hadn't actually gone over Coutinho's head to Tanaka, but it felt as if she had.

So she signed out a departmental Ford Escape and borrowed a ladder from Absalom, the fatherly Hawaiian man who ran the maintenance department. He hunted up some rags and rope.

The SRT's had better equipment, but Kimo might wonder why they were letting her use it. Absalom accompanied her to the parking lot to help her lash the ladder to her car.

"Not like that," said an unwelcome voice behind her. She didn't turn around. Neither did Absalom.

"Glad you're an expert on something," she told Callen.

"What's that mean?"

"As opposed to backing another cop up."

"Your attitude is going to get you killed

"In front of a witness yet," she said. "Smart."

"Absalom didn't hear nothing. Right, brah?"

Jenny glanced at the maintenance man and saw that Callen had called it right. Absalom stared into the distance, as if he had the parking lot to himself.

Okay, then.

With the ladder attached, she picked Kimo up at the curb and drove to the hole in the ground near his mother's house. Jenny disciplined her eyes as she navigated the familiar streets. Kimo might catch her checking the mirror for the men in black. But three-sixty awareness was a habit that she found hard to shut off.

She parked at the end of the street and let Kimo lead the way into the brush. The flat rocks were still scattered on the ground.

"You know who was messing with the religion?" she asked Kimo.

"No clue."

She let him lower the ladder and go down first. He stood in the small circle of natural light at the bottom of the tube as she tossed a Maglite down to him. Her own flashlight hung from her gear belt, which gave her the usual trouble when she executed an unfamiliar maneuver. Items on the belt snagged first on the top of the ladder and then on the edge of the hole. She finally landed on the floor of the tube without losing anything.

"Lead the way," she told Kimo.

He pointed in the opposite direction of the Otsaka house. This tube must be epic.

They walked for ten minutes. Kimo concentrated his beam on their footing, leaving Jenny free to play the light in all directions, looking for something that didn't belong.

"I remember this split," said Kimo.

"Which fork did you take?"

"We didn't. This is where she jumped me."

A puff of breeze came from one of the branches of the tube, and Jenny knew what this was all about.

8

"No, what?"

The sickly sweetness of ether and the scouring effect of ammonia mixed unpleasantly.

"Really?"

"I gotta quit smoking," said Kimo. "I can't smell much of nothing."

"Well, don't light up now."

Jenny went right up to the split. Her flashlight showed her nothing in the right fork, but in the left her beam picked out white plastic jugs lined up against one wall.

"Meth," said Jenny. "What I thought. Let's back out now."

• • •

Jenny emerged first from the ground. When Kimo followed her and found himself surrounded by tactical officers, he gave her a reproachful look.

"This wasn't a date," she told him. "I'm a cop."

Coutinho was standing nearby. He led Kimo off and spoke to him for several minutes. When he was through, the young man gave a minimal nod and walked off in the direction of his mother's house. Coutinho returned to Jenny.

"We'll have to question him some more, but I'm pretty sure he's clean."

"I am too. He didn't know what was going on down there."

"How does this play to you?"

"I think Cindy wanted a guide down there," said Jenny. "Which suggests she wasn't part of the meth ring, or she would already have known her way around."

"And once she found out what she needed to know, she jumped on Kimo to distract him."

"Glad I didn't have to do that."

"So what was her plan? And whose meth operation is it?"

"Now we know there was money to find," she said. "Just not in the form we were looking for."

"And right away Cindy started adapting her plans," said Coutinho.

"You know what else I'm wondering? Where did that breeze come from? It was in my face, not from behind.

Which means it didn't come from this entrance. If we can find that out, it might tell us something."

"Another entrance. Maybe. It could be too small to be useful, but we should look." Coutinho grinned. "Or you could just get lucky again."

• • •

It would make an interesting experiment. Could she make her own luck? Or was it more of a Zen thing than that?

For two days her routine calls kept her in Hilo, where finding undiscovered entrances to the subterranean world was less likely. If there was a hole big enough to fall into, or even just break an ankle, some civilian would already have found it the hard way. She ran into Coutinho several times before or after her middle shifts, which reminded her that his wife Lucy was doing her three long days at the crime lab in Honolulu. He was too preoccupied to do more than nod at Jenny as if he couldn't quite place her.

On the third day she was on her way from the locker room to roll call when he intercepted her.

"Can't find the source of that breeze yet. It could be quite a distance from the lab."

"It's a big island."

Hawaii County detectives told each other that when a case wasn't going well. Coutinho accepted the insight from her without reminding her that she wasn't a member of the detective club.

"I wouldn't mind finding some fingerprints, but every-thing in that lab is clean. Like they were really strict about wearing gloves, which smart bad guys would do for any number of reasons."

He blew air out.

"I hate it when they're smart."

•••

Dispatch sent Jenny to a vehicular accident on 130 outside Pahoa. An inattentive or arrogant motorist had T-boned an ancient pickup truck. Jenny assumed the offender was a visitor. Residents knew this island had room and time for everyone, and they hurried for no one.

She started directing traffic around the scene. She positioned three orange cones from her trunk and looked around. Right away the *malihini* theory began to fall apart. The offender had come out of the same subdivision where Jenny had been spending a lot of time on the Otsaka case. Not many visitors ventured off the highway into the unremarkable neighborhood.

On the other hand, the offending vehicle had disappeared. The local culture of obedience to authority would have kept most residents on the scene of an accident.

It shouldn't have surprised her that Jack Holloway was involved. The EMS ranks were even sparser than the police. He was working on the mostly Japanese man in his sixties who had been driving the pickup. Jack gave the man an ice pack to hold to his head and looped a blood pressure cuff around the man's bicep. Jenny approached. For the moment she had no traffic to direct.

"Howzit, Jack?"

"Howzit, Jenny."

"Hit and run?"

"Looks like it."

Gloves. Jack was wearing gloves.

Well, of course he was. Gloves were part of his job, but Jenny couldn't look away. Her mind was counting up the times she had seen Jack in gloves in recent days, all on occasions related to the Otsaka case.

Was this the luck she was supposed to be making? She hoped not, if it involved Jack.

She itched to get the story from the man under Jack's care, but his injuries were minor. She couldn't justify questioning him until Jack had finished with him. She also didn't want to alert Jack to her suspicions.

She hated thinking like this.

"Better get on it," said Jack.

His hands were full, but he nodded toward the highway. The respite from traffic was ending. Another ancient, overloaded truck going fifteen miles under the limit was leading a stately procession of vehicles. Jenny jogged to her position and started waving the drivers to the opposite shoulder.

Good thing she could handle business without thinking, because she had a lot to occupy her mind.

Back at the station she did a search and found what she didn't want to find. Six months earlier Cindy Montes had been involved in a fender bender in Captain Cook, south of Kona. One of the responding EMT's was a young woman Jenny didn't know, which stood to reason on the other side of the island.

The other was Jack Holloway. At some point he must have been lent to Kona Division or swapped assignments with someone over on that side of the island. Jenny hadn't been aware of it at the time, because she didn't monitor her exes like some women she knew.

She did know that the police frowned on Lone Ranger stuff. As much as she might want to investigate on her own, Coutinho needed to know what she had learned. It wouldn't be the first time her social life had benefitted his investigation.

She found him in the bullpen. He listened, and as usual he left her guessing at what was going on in his mind.

"You checked his social media?" he asked.

"He didn't post about any of this stuff."

"He's spent enough time around cops to know what's smart and what isn't."

He paused long enough to warn her what was coming.

"That means we're going to have to get somebody next to him."

Jenny stifled the protest that welled up in her throat. She should have seen this coming. Every cop was expected to put the job ahead of the personal.

"Have to figure out how to do it," she said instead.

If Coutinho replied something flippant, she was going to have a hard time controlling her response. But she shouldn't have doubted him.

"Got any ideas?" he asked.

"Yeah, I think I do."

• • •

As usual, Morrison knew when to play well with others, even cops. But he didn't have to like the assignment. His shoulders had a defensive hunch as he sat at the kitchen table in his house outside Pahoa.

Jenny hadn't seen this room before. Her night with Morrison had ended abruptly before he could give her breakfast. But these whitewashed island boxes varied little in their layout, and she could have found the kitchen blindfolded.

"I hate meth," he said.

"If this works," said Coutinho, "it might make a dent in the meth problem."

"Yeah, but you want me to look like a cooker."

"Just for the duration."

"I hope it doesn't get out."

"Nobody will hear it from us."

Jenny made three at the table. In this company she would usually have been standing against the wall in her uniform. Instead, she was channeling Morrison's latest hot young girlfriend in short shorts, tank top and sandals.

She missed the weight of her gun on her hip.

"I'm thinking you should get going," said Morrison.

Coutinho got up. The meeting was scheduled for midnight here in Morrison's kitchen. That was more than an hour away, but drug dealers were predictably paranoid.

The other parties to the deal would arrive early to scout the area. Coutinho turned toward Jenny.

"Yellow."

"Got it."

She remembered the color of the day from his first reminder, his second, and now his third. She didn't hold his obsessiveness against him.

•••

Jenny was expecting Jack, but the sight of him made his betrayal real and depressed her to the brink of tears. On the other hand, his companion got her adrenaline surging again.

"Well, lookit here," said Callen. "The golden girl ain't so golden."

"Fuck you," said Jenny.

She figured that was the right tone to take. Morrison laid a hand on her wrist. The gesture had just the right touch of ownership, which made her want to slap his hand away. She controlled the urge.

"This is business," he said.

"Why's she here at all?" Callen demanded.

"Because she's my retirement plan."

"What, she's taking over for you?"

"You catch on fast. Maybe we can get along."

"I dunno," said Callen. "All these years hearing Morrison is smart. Morrison never wants to do anything but paka-lolo. Morrison never wants to get too big or piss anybody off. Now all of a sudden you're into meth? Doesn't track."

"I don't think he catches on fast," said Jenny to Morrison. "From what I've seen, he never catches on at all."

She turned to Callen.

"Morrison just told you, there's gonna be a new boss."

"And you need the cash to buy him out. I get it. What I don't get is why we care. Why should we let you in?"

"Because you don't have a choice. I know about you now. But I can also do you some good."

"How?"

"You need it spelled out for you? I can send investigations off in the wrong direction."

"You mean Coutinho. You think you can keep fooling him?"

"You couldn't, but I can."

Jenny put her nastiest smile on. Callen returned it.

"Always wondered about you and him."

As if a liaison with a detective would be the only reason she refused to fall for a great catch like Callen.

As she slogged through the repulsive dialog, Jenny tried to monitor Jack's reactions. He was blinking once a minute, as if his heartbeat had dropped into the reptilian range. Jenny would have bet he was thinking about the choices that had brought him here and wondering how he could back up and take a different path.

She couldn't help him with that.

"There's a problem, though," said Morrison. "We hear you had a setback. Your facility got taken down the other day."

"That's the kind of thing I can prevent," said Jenny.

Callen waved their words away.

"That's all part of the business model. We're up and running again already."

"Prove it," said Morrison.

Jenny thought quickly and approved. It didn't look as if Jack would say a word here in the kitchen. If she could separate him from Callen, she might get him talking. An excursion might give her the chance.

"Sure," said Callen. "But we have to go to Kona."

• • •

The Kona side had lava tubes as well. It figured. Volcanoes had created the entire island. In the first light of the day Jenny could see vast fields of flat black rock in every direction. The view was one reason she wondered how people could live here. On the Hilo side, the rainforest concealed the bones of the island like the body of a beautiful woman.

Morrison drove one of his Jeeps, this one a Cherokee. He seemed to change them like his boxer shorts.

Which she had also seen.

Jack sat beside him in the front passenger seat, which put Callen to her right in the back. Jenny knew their destination, although she didn't have time to figure out the source of her certainty. Right now the problem of smoothing Callen's paranoia demanded her full attention.

"Aren't you on early shift?" he demanded.

If she turned around right now, she would still be hours late for roll call.

"I'm with Coutinho for now. Sarge isn't happy, but he's used to that."

"And Coutinho trusts you?"

"That's what this is all about."

"Maybe you're wired."

"Maybe you want to try and find out."

In fact, she was wearing a wire, but she couldn't have him finding out. She turned her head to stare him down, and she loved how it felt.

But the hard part of the job was Jack, who hadn't spoken at all in the hours since they had left Pahoa.

Morrison looked alert and self-contained. Jenny compared her father's recent habit of yawning at nine PM, and Daddy was ten years younger than Morrison. She hoped she could preserve that kind of stamina into her sixties.

Several miles short of Kona Morrison slowed the vehicle. He turned left and pulled into the parking lot of Hanson's coffee warehouse. He sent all the windows down and shut the engine off. The silence of the world's largest ocean, never far away, invaded the vehicle like a ninja army. The rush hour would start soon, but now nothing distracted Jenny from her own heartbeat.

Callen was the first to break under the enormous nothingness. Jenny wasn't surprised.

"Ready for the tour?"

Jenny climbed out and waited. Her plan was to stick close to Jack and try to get him alone long enough to make him talk.

Callen led the party along the south side of the

corrugated steel building. Six feet past the end of the structure he stopped.

"Good thing I'm such a nice guy," he said. "I could have just let you keep going."

He turned a flashlight on and played the beam along the ground. Eight or ten feet of rocky footing ended abruptly in blackness.

"Must be quite a drop there," said Morrison.

"Over a hundred feet straight down," said Callen. "This way."

He led them south along the cliff for a hundred yards that felt like miles. Callen stopped, and again his beam crept along the ground and disappeared into blackness. But this pocket of void was only a couple of feet square.

"Check it out."

Everyone came close. Callen showed them a ladder leading down.

"Just broke through recently. There's a big tube down there, and it's perfect. Natural ventilation from a big opening in the cliff. The wind never stops blowing here, and that takes care of the cooking odors. This facility is going to last us quite a while. Weirdest thing, though. We found some bones in it. Right at the opening. What's that about?"

He didn't wait for an answer. For a moment Jenny pictured lava pouring out of the sea cliff directly into the ocean however many centuries or millennia ago. Then she saw a Hawaiian warrior rappelling down the cliff to store the bones of a chief in the lava tube. Their location would remain secret for centuries, after the warrior hurled himself to his death on the rocks below.

And now an ignorant drug dealer had defiled the sacrifice. Callen needed to pay with a deadly fall of his own.

She shook the useless thought off and concentrated on this entrance to the tube. A man Morrison's size would scrape his shoulders on both sides of the hole. In the dim ambient light he looked displeased.

"No way are my partner and I both going down there. One of us stays here with one of you."

In fact, no one was going down there. Jenny stifled a moment of regret. It would have been a great way to get Jack alone and press him for a confession, but it would also cut her off from her backup. Even if she lived to climb back out of the hole, Coutinho might kill her for going in.

Callen's recorded words would tie him to whatever the cops found in the tube. They would have to get the evidence for their murder cases some other way.

Jenny expected Callen to urge them down the ladder, but he stood silently and waited for something. She looked toward Morrison and realized she could see his outline without a flashlight. They had just a few minutes of darkness left. Was that good or bad?

As she turned her eyes back to Callen, she caught the moment when a rock flying out of the darkness struck him a brutal blow in the face. He staggered backward and disappeared over the cliff. Jenny flinched and waited for his scream to reach her and fade as he fell, but maybe the missile had mercifully knocked him out.

And who was this man striding into view from the south? The silhouette had the body language of a young man. Jenny snapped her own flashlight on and played it on his face. The stark light altered his features, and she needed a moment to recall challenging him with a boy-girl look in the coffee warehouse.

9

"WE DIDN'T MEET properly the other day," the young man said. "I'm Ralph. I know. I don't look like a Ralph. Everybody tells me that."

"Jenny," she said. "I guess you're what a Ralph looks like."

Participating in the demented dialog gave her a moment to think.

"You're welcome," he said.

"For what?"

"Getting rid of your problem."

For another crazy moment Jenny though he meant sexual harassment in the police department. How could he know about that?

"One cop in this operation is enough," he said. "Two would trip over each other. The way he just did over his own feet. Who knows what the hell he was doing here. Right?"

"I'll try not to be a problem."

"Good idea."

"Was Cindy a problem?"

Where had that come from? Maybe it was just the contrast between Ralph and Jack. The role of killer had never sat well on Jack, but this new young man had just proved himself.

"She was a pain in the ass from the beginning."

Jenny started to ask how Cindy had wedged her way into the operation, but that question would have to wait until she could act like a cop again. Right now she was a bad guy.

"Ready to see the facilities?"

"No, we're good," said Morrison.

Jenny blessed him, but Ralph gave him a suspicious look.

"You came all this way, and now you take my word for it?"

"My nose works," said Jenny.

Just in time a puff of air brought the odors of meth from the hole in the ground.

"Well, that's awkward," said Ralph.

His right hand held a compact Glock.

And now Ralph's plan hit Jenny all at once—get them all underground and kill them where no one would ever find them. Then become Mr. Pakalolo as well as Mr. Meth.

"Three of you all fall off the cliff?" said Ralph. "That

raises some questions. But as long as there's nothing to connect you with me …"

"Yellow," said Jenny.

"Who's yellow?"

She pictured Coutinho telling the tactical officers, "Go, go, go!" But she couldn't afford to wait for them. They had some ground to cover.

Her chances didn't look good. The rough ground could trip her a half dozen times as she tried to charge Ralph. The footing didn't really matter, because distance would have been too far to cover even on flat pavement.

But she had to try.

"Think you're going to help yourself to my pakalolo operation?" Morrison asked.

From his tone they could have been discussing the matter in Luquin's over drinks.

"That's the plan," said Ralph."

"Think I don't have safeguards?"

"I don't care."

Ralph turned back to Jenny, and his gun hand started to rise.

"Ralph, what are you doing back here?"

It took Jenny a moment to place the voice. Then Hanson, the warehouse owner, appeared above them. Ralph's head turned toward him. Jenny launched herself, but it was no good. Ralph's gun hand didn't waver. Even worse, she tripped and sprawled on the stony ground. Her mind flashed uselessly back to Langston Otsaka's backyard. This case was giving her knees a beating.

Then the crisp brutality of a rifle round made her forget her bruises. Her stalling had allowed her backup to get close.

And somehow she knew the sound of that rifle. Nobody beat Patsy with a long gun, not even the men in black. Coutinho had kicked some ass to get Patsy included in the team.

Jenny stopped grinning as she watched Ralph writhing and moaning the ground. If he was in pain, he was alive, and the cops would get to question him.

Hanson joined her. The sight of his employee seemed to fascinate and repel him at the same time.

"Next time I find something in my warehouse," he said, "I think I'm going to keep my mouth shut."

"I hope you don't, but I wouldn't blame you."

• • •

"Like I said, Cindy was a pain in the ass," said Ralph, "but I didn't kill her."

He lay handcuffed to his hospital bed in Kona Community Hospital. The facility was new to Jenny, but she had already mapped out a coffee route for after the interview.

She waited for Coutinho to pick up the questioning, but he left it to her.

"Don't even try it," she said. "We're supposed to believe you didn't take out somebody trying to muscle in on your meth operation? We already know how you react to problems."

"Okay, I probably would have killed her, but somebody beat me to it."

"Jack?"

"I doubt it. He was useless about that stuff."

"So what good was he?"

"He's a good chemist. Gotta give him that. Nothing ever blew up on his watch."

She probed some more, but her efforts yielded nothing. And she knew she was only postponing the task of putting what she knew into words. This time she led the coffee expedition, and Coutinho followed. She bought two coffees and got cream and sugar for herself, whether the detective approved or not.

"What's on you mind, Officer?"

She should just stop trying to conceal her thinking from him.

"I hate this, but I believe him about Cindy."

"So do I."

Neither needed to say more. Jenny wasn't even sure how she knew. They took their time over their coffee, but then they had to start the drive around the island. The trip had never seemed longer, and Jenny had never been less eager to see it end.

Mrs. Conyers opened the door as if she had been waiting. Maybe she had.

"Officer Freitas. You brought your friend."

Jenny stifled an urge to look sideways at Coutinho. Were they friends? She had never thought about it.

"Come."

To the kitchen, of course. They took the same seats as last time, and in the same order, with Jenny the last to remain on her feet.

"You know."

Jenny waited a beat, but Coutinho was leaving it to her.

"Yes, Auntie, we know."

"Some people just shouldn't come back home. She was no good to begin with. The mainland made her worse."

Jenny didn't need it spelled it out. In her mind she saw the scattered stones of the traditional religious observance, and heard the auntie's words,

"I see the old religion doing the young men some good."

But she needed the complete story for the case record, even if she expected Mrs. Conyers to plead out instead of going to trial.

"Am I right that she came back and wormed her way into your life?"

"Couldn't stop her, even when I knew what she was doing. She could manipulate like nobody else I know."

"Including helping herself to your son?"

"He's a grown man, but he's still a boy. If you know what I mean."

"Did Cindy ruin the shrine?"

"That I don't know, but it would make sense. She just lived to wreck things."

Spreading meth among the islands certainly qualified.

"So how did it happen?"

"She showed up at my door, hurting bad."

"Did she say what happened?"

"She fell. Didn't tell me where or how."

Jenny and Coutinho exchanged looks. Cindy had been the champion *tita* of all time, if she could drive back to Hilo with the injuries she must have suffered in the fall in Hanson's warehouse.

"She was sitting right where you are. Just assuming I would drop everything to help her again. All of a sudden I was sick and tired of it. I got up like I was going to make tea. Heals, all, right? But then I hit her with my best cast iron skillet. Had to get a kahuna to say some words over it before I could use it again."

Mrs. Conyers fixed Jenny with a look.

"Yes, I'm a Baptist. But this is also Hawaii."

• • •

Internal Affairs spent days fawning over Jenny, not that a civilian would have recognized their hours of questioning as deference. Hilo Division borrowed detectives from Kona with the official explanation that they would be more objective. But the IA investigators were pulling their punches. Callen had been a wrong cop all along, and the Hilo brass could have listened to Jenny and other women officers and saved the department a lot of trouble.

Now they were trying to talk her out of suing the department without actually mentioning the word "sue."

It was a good thing they were treating her gently, because the better half of her brain insisted on working the Otsaka case.

An IA detective named Rivera had just worked his way

up to the bar fight that Callen and Dumas had let Jenny handle alone.

"Yeah," said Jenny. "I was getting my ass kicked, and the brotherhood in blue was leaning against the wall."

She was enjoying the latitude to be crude that her position gave her this once, but something was interfering with the simple pleasures.

What was bothering her? She narrowed it down to the last phrase she had uttered.

Brotherhood. Brother. Brothers.

It gnawed at her but refused to come.

Until that night in bed, when she had one of her insomniac episodes. Sometime around first light she dozed off.

And came awake minutes later to the echo of Caleb Otsaka's voice in her mind.

"Sometimes he would call me Abel."

And everybody in these biblical islands knew what happened to Abel.

●●●

"Another son? Whose?"

"Most likely Cindy's in Vegas."

"How did Langston know about him?"

"Maybe he came looking for Langston like everybody else. And for the same reason."

"The famous money."

Coutinho thought about it.

"We need to place somebody else in Langston's back

yard, but let's not get ahead of ourselves. Let's find out if Abel is real."

"It would help if there was somebody we could talk to who's still alive."

"You're hard to please."

• • •

Sometimes Jenny was glad to leave the detective stuff to the detectives, generally when she saw no way forward with the case. Then the daily routine of a patrol officer regained its rookie fascination.

She answered lost cat calls and broke up the usual bar fights. And she took the never-ending burglary reports from visitors who left valuables in their rental cars.

This call came from a Hilo resident complaining about glass from a broken car window littering the street. Jenny found the Ford Focus still parked amid the shards, which didn't look right. She walked around the car and inspected it. The license plate bracket belonged to a local company with a record of laxity on little things like verifying the identity of the customer.

While Jenny checked the seats through the windows, a man appeared around the corner. His two hundred plus pounds didn't stand out in these islands, but his black suit and thousand-dollar loafers did. He hesitated, but she looked straight at him to make it clear she had seen him and connected him with the vehicle. He gave up on his idea of escaping and approached her.

"Your car?"

"That's right, Officer. I already called the company."

"But not the police."

"What's the point?"

"Reporting a crime is the point. Where are you from?"

"Vegas."

"Can I see some ID, please?"

"Why?"

"Because I'm the police, and I asked to see ID."

And because she wasn't a hick. Like his car, the man just didn't look right.

He stared at her until her gun hand tingled. Was he really going to start something on the street in Hilo? That kind of thing didn't fly even in Vegas.

"Now, please."

She watched his hands as they went into his pocket and emerged with a wallet. A moment later she was reading his Nevada drivers license. Carl Fortunato in the flesh matched his DMV photo. She made him watch as she recorded his information in her notebook.

"What's missing from the car?"

"They're welcome to my dirty underwear."

"How about the guns?"

That was a guess, but his stony expression confirmed it.

"You need permits in Hawaii."

"What for? Didn't have any guns."

She thought about telling him that the cops had been expecting someone like him to come for Caleb Otsaka, but she decided against revealing everything she knew.

She handed his license back.

"Enjoy your stay."

He could have been a little more gracious about turning away.

"The other shoe," said Coutinho when she told him about the encounter.

"We don't really have anything on him," said Jenny.

"He as much as confessed to bringing a gun. As close as the wise guys ever get to giving it up."

"He also doesn't have to be here for Caleb. He could be WITSEC himself."

Urban folklore held that this island was one of the witness protection program's favorite places to stash people. There was no way to verify the proposition, but it seemed plausible. The Big Island had a limited number of entry points for the U.S. Marshals to watch for potential assassins, and anyone they wanted to protect could blend into the multi-ethnic population..

"If it's Caleb they want, he's making it easy for them, dropping out of the program and using his own name."

"I think we can get Fortunato where we want him," said Jenny.

Coutinho caught right on.

"Through the guns."

"I'll get Nate on it," she said.

"And I'll call Vegas about Fortunato."

Jenny went to her Camry drove the short distance to the no-name bar, where she spent ten minutes sitting in the parking lot. Several mokes looked sideways at her before they went in. The island telegraph would take it from there.

Ten minutes later Nate climbed into her back seat.

"Nate, here's how you earn some points with us."

"Don't need no points."

"You know you will."

His tough guy act made her feel tired, but she slogged onward.

"Somebody just got his hands on a gun. Maybe a couple of guns. We want them."

"Okay."

"This is serious, Nate. We know these guns are out there. Anybody tries to use them is in big trouble. That includes selling them."

"I get it."

It took two more days, but then Nate found her in the same parking lot. He made such a production of looking around before ducking into her back seat that every moke in Hilo probably noticed. Jenny drove around the corner and parked. Nate leaned forward.

"I got your guns."

10

"YOU GOT MY GUNS?"

Jenny felt stupid for the repetition, but it was unlike Nate to get results so efficiently.

"Well, I don't have them on me."

That was more like it.

"This friend of mine thinks he's gonna get paid."

"How?"

"Says he's got two nine-mills. He's gonna keep one and sell the other back to the moke."

"Who's this friend?"

"Petey Kawabata."

"Petey's in over his head," said Jenny.

She could say that without knowing the details. Like Nate, Petey was usually in over his head the moment he got out of bed, but he refused to learn.

"How's he going to make the deal?"

"Friend of his at the car company got word to the *malihini* rented the vehicle."

It figured that this rental company would have somebody like that.

"They got a meet set up for tonight."

"Where's Petey?"

Nate pointed toward the bar with his chin.

"Where else he gonna be?"

"Thanks, Nate. You did good."

Jenny waited for Nate to climb out and called Coutinho again.

"I'm thinking we'll wire Kenny and send him to the meet," he said.

"That works."

Kenny Lujan couldn't relax off duty in a tank top and board shorts without mainland visitors sidling up to him and asking where they could get some of that good island pakalolo. The man from Vegas would take him for a sketchy local guy.

"Kenny should bring backup," said Jenny. "A real moke would."

"That's a no-brainer. Sammy."

The door to the bar opened.

"Here comes Petey. Bets on where he goes?"

"He's going home," said Coutinho. "Petey's not smart enough to keep the guns anywhere else. I'll meet you there."

And when Coutinho pounded on the door to the

apartment, Petey opened with his hapless expression already in place. He knew from experience what cops sounded like when they knocked. Coutinho had his stern father look on, although he didn't have children of his own. Jenny gave Petey a little credit for catching on right away. He could give up the guns and slide on the charges related to breaking into the rental car. And he could stay alive. Dealing with the mob wouldn't have gone the way he hoped.

In less than five minutes Jenny was carrying two nine-millimeter Glocks out to her car.

"It'll be interesting to trace them," said Coutinho.

But now their task was to catch the man from Vegas in a transaction for illegal guns.

"I'll go put the fear of God into the rental company," said Coutinho. "Maybe this will make them clean up their act. For a while, anyway."

According to Petey, Fortunato had agreed to come to the parking lot of Lava Trees State Park outside Pahoa. Jenny wondered whether the mainlander knew what he was getting into. In Las Vegas darkness was theoretical. In Lava Trees the entire police department could lurk unseen just beyond the glow from the restroom building.

Kenny was jumpy, but that fit the character he was playing. Sammy was Sammy, always and everywhere, but his stoic front made him the perfect bodyguard. Coutinho had found them an ancient Wrangler to drive to the meet. Jenny couldn't detect the vehicle's color under its authentic coating of red Big Island mud.

She dawdled outside the locker room after the middle shift. She was about to conclude that Coutinho didn't plan to take her on this midnight expedition, when he found her and told her to get into the black Ford Excursion with four members of the Special Response Team. The men in black didn't talk to her, but they didn't kick her out of the vehicle, either.

The park closed after dark, but access was easy. So was staking out the meeting. Jenny found a place behind one of the stone pillars that gave the place its name. During one of the many volcanic eruptions that had made this island, an *ohi'a* tree, wet from the constant rains, had cooled the lava abruptly enough to create a stone pillar that remained after the rest of the flow moved on. Centuries later the pillar towered over her, and she didn't have to get down prone or even risk grass stains on the knees of her uniform trousers.

The night mist soaked her before she noticed it, but on this island the moisture warmed her. A Hilo native expected to get wet anyway.

The Wrangler lurched into the lot. Jenny approved of Kenny's method acting. The vehicle parked, and the lights cut off. Jenny waited for her night vision to return and resolved to look away from Fortunato's headlights when he drove in.

He arrived just five minutes later. Jenny closed her eyes before she could make out what kind of car the rental company had given him. When she looked again, Kenny and Sammy had climbed out to meet him. They left their doors open to keep the courtesy light on.

"Hell of a way to treat a guest on your island," said Fortunato.

"What kind of guest brings guns?"

Jenny grinned in the dark. That kind of improvisation showed a new side of Sammy.

"I want them back."

"It'll cost you, and we're keeping one of them."

"The hell you are. I got a sniper with a bead on you."

"The hell you do."

"Think there's only two guns on this island?"

Something had been lurking just out of sight in Jenny's mind, and now it stepped into view. Why was Fortunato undertaking this expedition into unfamiliar territory alone? She had heard stories about mob assassinations. If he was here to kill Caleb, shouldn't he have a driver and a spotter to confirm the target?

"We can do this easy, or we can do it hard," said Kenny. "Easy is you give us five bills and we give you your gun. Hard, you don't want to know. This is our territory."

Jenny could almost feel the man seething.

"Deal. But if you ever come to Vegas, we'll talk again."

Fortunato reached into his back pocket and removed something. It could have been an envelope. Kenny took it from him and lifted the flap to check the contents.

"Five hundred George Washingtons," he said.

The first president was the signal.

"Go," said Coutinho somewhere nearby.

Powerful flashlight beams criss-crossed and settled on the group of four.

"Police! Don't move!"

Fortunato's reaction confirmed the many arrests in his file. He knew what to do when cops bellowed in unison. He froze and then followed each order until he wore the handcuffs.

Coutinho turned to Jenny.

"You take the gentleman in my car. I'll ride with the SRT's."

The tactic was routine. Male suspects sometimes let things slip with Jenny, but Fortunato probably had rides with women cops on his resume along with everything else. He let the trip to Kapiolani Street pass in silence.

It was almost two in the morning—detective hours. Coutinho performed the booking chores and stowed Fortunato in Interview Two.

"I'll give him an hour and go in," said Coutinho, "but it won't make any difference."

Jenny was able to catch up on a couple of patrol reports. Then it was time to test Coutinho's prediction. She watched the laptop screen, as Fortunato invoked his rights. Coutinho rejoined Jenny in the bullpen.

"Did your friend in Vegas give you anything?" she asked.

"He said there are rumors Fortunato is not the earner he used to be. He's kind of on probation."

Coutinho shook his head in unison.

"Costing the mob money used to be fatal. What are we coming to?"

Jenny suspected a deadpan joke, but she let it go.

"So maybe that's why they sent him to take Caleb out," she said. "To give him a chance to get right with the bosses."

"And he just blew it. He might not want to go home."

The commotion started around the corner and grew louder. The noise appeared in the form of Agnes Rodrigues.

"Who else?" said Coutinho.

Jenny expected him to look even more exhausted, but he seemed to perk up. Jenny grinned. Coutinho would never admit it, but he would miss Rodrigues when he retired. She would miss him too.

But then something occurred to Jenny.

"How did he know to get Rodrigues?"

"Maybe he did his homework before he came here."

Coutinho didn't sound as if he had convinced himself. But then Typhoon Agnes made landfall.

"Where is my client?"

Fortunato's image was clear on Coutinho's laptop screen, which suggested Rodrigues didn't know him.

"Nice to see you too, Counselor."

Coutinho never let the lawyer see him sweat. Rodrigues ignored the pleasantry.

"Interview Two," he said.

Rodrigues turned and marched. Jenny noted that she trusted Coutinho to mute the sound. Some detectives she wouldn't.

Someone came up behind Jenny.

"What do we have?" Rebecca Cordova asked.

She looked as fresh as she did during office hours. Jenny felt a need to check herself in the mirror to make sure she was keeping up appearances. Inside she was starting to drag.

Coutinho told Cordova about the night's activities.

"I'm thinking this could get Federal," said Coutinho. "He's going to want WITSEC. The Vegas mob won't be in a forgiving mood."

"Let's make sure before we wake up a U.S. Attorney," said Cordova.

It took almost an hour, but Rodrigues came out and said, "My client wishes to speak with you."

Cordova tossed her chin in a "Let's go" kind of gesture. She aimed it at Coutinho, who turned and performed the same choreography with Jenny. Cordova stopped for a moment, as if she wanted to make an issue of Jenny's inclusion, but she decided to maintain a united front for Rodrigues.

Inside, Jenny stood against the wall. No one was going to fetch a chair for her. She turned her attention to Fortunato, who wasn't looking desperate for a deal. He looked more like a man with four aces.

Rodrigues nodded at her client.

"I want to walk on these bullshit charges," said Fortunato.

"In Hawaii gun charges aren't bullshit," said Coutinho. "I'm guessing you care even more about murder."

"What murder?" Cordova asked.

"Caleb Otsaka."

"He's alive."

"You want to keep him that way, you talk to me."

"Are you here to kill him?"

"My client wants immunity on conspiracy and attempted murder charges," said Rodrigues.

"Well, since he screwed that up anyway, we can let it slide."

Rodrigues nodded her approval at Fortunato, who glowered at Cordova's insult until his lawyer nudged him.

"I'm not the only one after him. There's a freelancer in the picture. He got in my way, which is why I didn't pull the job off."

Jenny could have mentioned that leaving his guns vulnerable to theft had also contributed, but Cordova knew the story already.

"So who are we looking for?"

"All I know is, Abel something. From Vegas."

"That's not worth immunity," said Cordova.

"It's more than you had. You didn't know he existed."

Cordova glanced at Coutinho, who pointed at the door with her eyes. The prosecutor got up.

"Excuse us a moment."

Jenny followed them out into the hall.

"Did we know anything about this Abel?"

Coutinho deferred to Jenny.

"Caleb Otsaka said his father called him Abel once in

a while. He thought it was age-related confusion. So did we."

"It didn't occur to you that there was a real Abel to confuse him with?"

"Maybe it should have," said Coutinho.

Cordova's reprimand didn't seem to ruffle him.

"I'll call Vegas," he said.

"And I'll stall Rodrigues," said Cordova.

Everyone knew who had the harder assignment.

Coutinho beckoned to Jenny and started toward his office. He waved her toward his partner's vacant chair. Jenny's eyes went to the wall clock, which read five o'clock.

"Eight A.M. in Vegas," he said.

He picked up the phone on his desk and a moment later was deep in conversation with his detective contact.

"He's going to call back with the latest info," he said after ending the call, "but he told me right off—the cops know Abel Montes. Very bad boy, apparently."

"That's the name Cindy was using there."

"It is," said Coutinho. "All that trash talk about how horrible motherhood is—we never even considered that she might have done it twice."

"Was he Langston's son?"

"That we'll have to find out. But Langston obviously knew him, or knew of him."

"I'll bet he's here right now."

"Like every other troublemaker on the planet."

Coutinho breathed in and out a few times.

"A self-pity party is fun once in a while, but that's

enough for now. While we're waiting on Vegas, let's see what else we can get from Fortunato. Agnes will love it."

As always, the thought of his favorite adversary seemed to improve his mood. He looked at the clock.

"I'll handle that. Roll call soon."

And with that Jenny remembered the patrol shift that stretched ahead of her on zero sleep. For a moment resentment flared. She was twenty-seven years old, not some college kid.

But she told herself to let it go. Detectives put in these hours all the time, and she needed to learn how.

11

AFTER FOUR YEARS on the job Jenny knew how to tune the radio out until it said something she needed to hear. This time Dispatch was patching Patsy through.

"Got a possible on that BOLO.".

Patsy was back in Hilo too, now that the brass had no need to camouflage Jenny's exile to Kona. Patsy recited an address in Langston Otsaka's neighborhood.

Jenny knew the place. Abel must be staying with her old friend Hez Kekua.

"En route," she said.

She was turning into Otsaka's street when the radio spoke up again.

"Suspect is on the move," said Patsy. "Red Wrangler. I'm about to do a stop."

"You need backup on this one," said Jenny.

She was probably closest, and she didn't plan to wait for Dispatch to make it official. She cut a U-turn and floored the accelerator.

But close wasn't close enough. Adrenaline flared when Jenny rounded the corner and saw Patsy flat on the blacktop next to her Malibu with the blue cone on the roof.

"Officer down."

A tiny corner of Jenny's mind congratulated her on the level tone of her voice. The more stressful the moment, the more a cop strove for professional detachment. She turned the flasher on and parked behind Patsy's vehicle. Jenny got out and drew her service weapon. No one else was in sight, but a chain link fence flanking the road needed clearing. It was draped with the usual vines and creepers, which could conceal an attacker. She led with her gun as she approached and ventured a quick look over the fence.

Nothing. She leaned over the fence again and scanned the whole area. Now she could go to her friend. Patsy was drawing her knees up in preparation to roll over and get to her feet.

"Stay, girlfriend," said Jenny.

"Moke is quick," said Patsy. "Never saw it coming."

She felt her jaw.

"Where you hurting?" Jenny asked.

"He punched me in the face. And I hit the back of my head on the car on the way down. Don't even remember doing that, but I must have."

Sirens were sounding. Kenny Lujan was the first to arrive, with Sammy seconds behind him. Then came

Sergeant Silveira just ahead of an ambulance. Jenny suppressed a pang when she noticed that Jack Holloway was missing from the EMT crew.

In the press of uniforms a large man in a tank top and board shorts stood out.

"Howzit, Officer?"

"Howzit, Hez."

"She gonna be okay?"

"I think so. How long has he been around?"

"Abel? Been on the island a few weeks, but he came to me a couple of days ago. Told me his last place fell through. He ain't a moke you tell no."

"You didn't think to tell us?"

"I'll punch it out with anybody, Officer. But Abel skips the fists and goes straight to his knife."

"How do you know him?"

"I was in Vegas for a while, trying to get in with the casinos. My cousin knew Abel. Not that he was happy about it."

"What brought Abel here?"

"What else? Langston's money."

"Did he mention anybody else he knows here?"

"He said about six words to me. Just drank my beer and ate my grindz."

"Okay Hez. If he turns up again, this time you call."

"If I can do it without getting stuck."

Coutinho was just climbing out of his Camry. He spoke with Patsy as she sat in the rear of the ambulance and then listened to Jenny's report.

"Abel believes in the money too," she finished.

They stood there thinking like a couple of detectives.

"I'm guessing he had a backup place to go," said Coutinho.

"Guys like that usually pick on a woman."

Coutinho looked sideways at her, but he didn't dispute her conclusion.

"He started out here only knowing Hez," she said, "but he'd have been planning to move on to something better."

As a cop with her share of domestic calls, Jenny knew which women were in no position to say no to a man. Waitresses. Bartenders. Hookers.

Even as stressful a situation as an officer down ended with Jenny back on patrol. An hour later she was driving the length of Banyan Drive looking for anything out of place on Hilo's prime hotel and restaurant strip.

Sally Pineda wasn't exactly out of place in her tank top, short shorts and high-heeled sandals. Hotels were her natural habitat, but Jenny decided to lower Sally's comfort level a little. She pulled over to the shoulder and stopped facing the wrong way. It didn't make much difference, because traffic was light, and street parking was always available on Banyan. Visitors sometimes remarked on the pleasant reminder of what life on all the islands used to be like.

Jenny rolled her window down.

"Howzit, Sally?"

"Howzit, Officer."

"What happened to your eye?"

"Ran into a door."

"Come on. You can do better than that. Was it Rodney?"

Her longtime boyfriend/pimp.

"Ain't with Rodney no more."

"But you're still doing this."

Jenny waved at the hotels.

"Girl's gotta make a living."

"So who's the new Rodney?"

It would never occur to Sally to get free of Rodneys in general.

"Abel."

Could it really be that easy? Jenny probed, and the man with the fists sounded like the one the police were looking for.

"Where's Abel now?"

"You asking me to roll on my man?"

"You want some time to think about it? In a cell?"

"You got nothing on me."

"Don't embarrass yourself, Sally. You've got warrants."

Jenny hadn't checked, but Sally's reaction confirmed the guess.

"He's at my place."

"Where you staying these days?"

"Out past the blacktop."

Cops always took the Special Response Team out that way, even when their objective wasn't as dangerous as Abel Montes. Aloha for the police was in short supply.

Jenny called Coutinho.

"Got lucky again."

"Don't knock it," he said. "Come back and join the fun."

By the time she reached headquarters, Coutinho had assembled a team of six men in black plus Patsy with a rifle. Jenny had the impression that her friend was going to find herself included in more of these missions. Patsy's smile said, "Bring it on."

"Guess there's no concussion," said Jenny.

"Nah, I'm good to go."

As everyone packed into the Ford Bronco, the SRT's accepted Patsy as one of them, but they eyed Jenny with skepticism.

Stealth was impossible. Every inhabitant of this neighborhood had eyes for the cops, and no one would keep quiet. Only speed would work.

The Bronco spun off mud as it roared down the center of the road. It slid to a stop in front of Sally's house, which, like many dwellings here, wasn't much more than a shack. The men in black piled out and made straight for the only door. Patsy jumped out and cut to the right, where she surveyed the neighborhood with her rifle pointed at the mud for now.

Last came Coutinho with the no-knock warrant, and Jenny.

The first man through the door tested the knob. It turned, as Sally had promised.

The operation didn't take long. Three minutes later the men in black came out with a young man in handcuffs. Abel Montes smiled tolerantly, as if a neighbor had asked a favor at an inconvenient moment.

Now the Bronco was really crowded. Jenny sat in the third row, crushed between two large men. Since she had nothing to do but ride, she studied the back of Abel's head for clues to his thoughts. His face wouldn't have revealed anything more.

No one spoke the entire trip.

Coutinho followed the detective manual and put Abel alone in an interview room to marinate in his own anxiety. It worked with suspects who felt anxious to begin with, but this one gave the impression that he hadn't even cried as an infant. Coutinho, Jenny and the prosecutor Cordova watched the young man on Coutinho's laptop screen. The three of them filled his tiny office.

"I'm not going to get anything," said Coutinho, "but I have to show the flag."

"Let Freitas try," said Cordova.

Jenny fought an urge to turn and gape at the prosecutor. When had this woman become a fan? Coutinho nodded as if he had been about to suggest the same thing.

"Okay," said Cordova, "what's the plan?"

"Play up to him," said Coutinho. "You have the equipment. Use it."

The female equipment. Jenny told herself that a man who let his hormones put him in prison deserved what he got, but the whole idea still left a bad taste.

Coutinho handed her a file folder.

"From my friend in Las Vegas."

Abel's file was extensive, if short on arrests and convictions. Local bad guys dropped dark hints about his part in heists and extortions, but they refused to say more. Their fear of this young man clung to the scanned and printed pages like greasy fingerprints.

"Game face," said Cordova.

That was usually Coutinho's line.

Jenny nodded and pushed through the door. The young man eyed her flagrantly up and down.

"I love this island."

The smirk on his handsome face changed the plan in an instant. Abel Montes was used to getting over on women. Jenny decided to play it like the only woman on earth who didn't buy his act. She thought he might take her as a challenge, but if she failed, Cordova would rip her a new one. Coutinho would defend her, and that would feel even worse.

Jenny took her seat across from him. Abel reminded her of a certain A-list Hollywood actor who was supposed to make her heart flutter but didn't.

"So what brought you back here?"

He opened his mouth for another smart remark. Jenny held up her hand.

"Wait."

She had two reasons to read him the Miranda warning. He was in custody, and she wanted to control the rhythm of the interview.

"You were going to say?"

"I wanted to get back to my roots. Mom told me a lot."

"About your father?"

"My father was in Vegas."

"Who was he?"

"He's dead."

The short answer threatened to become silence. Jenny dropped the question for now.

"So what did she tell you?"

"The usual. It's paradise. Nobody works too hard. Not as hot as Vegas."

"How about your brother?"

"Didn't know I had one until just recently. Mom talks a lot, but she doesn't always say much."

Jenny could corroborate that. And now she could identify the source of her wrong-footed feeling. Abel's voice echoed his mother's, and her personality animated his face in a way that didn't happen with her other son. This young man had grown up in Cindy's gravitational field.

"How did you find out about Caleb?"

"She decided to tell me."

"So she spills something like this that she could have told you anytime in the past twenty years? How did you handle that?"

"The way I handled everything she did. I could take it or leave it. I usually took it."

"You're very well known in Vegas."

"That's one way to put it."

"Was it getting too hot for you there?"

"It's always hot."

"You know what I mean."

"I can't speak to that. My lawyer back home would kick my ass."

Jenny didn't intend to ask about his lawyer on this island, if he had one. She Who Must Not Be Named, aka Agnes Rodrigues, might arise from the grimy floor of this very room in a cloud of infernal smoke.

"What did your mother want you to do here?"

"Nothing."

"We have witnesses to put you at Langston Otsaka's house. More than once. More than twice."

"I didn't know anybody here. He was somebody to look up if I needed anything."

Jenny decided it wasn't time to spring the topic of Langston's money on him.

"You strike me as pretty self-sufficient. What did you need from Langston?"

"I slept on his couch a couple of nights."

"How did you introduce yourself?"

"Friend of a friend."

"What friend?"

"I forget."

"So how did you end up in the warehouse?"

Her change-up didn't faze him. He had done this kind of thing before.

"Don't know what you're talking about."

"Don't try it. We found your prints up there in your man cave. You like beef jerky, I guess. I think it's disgusting."

"It's okay. Haven't had it in a while."

"Your mother understood what you like. She knows men, doesn't she?"

"What are you saying?"

"She knows how to get what she wants. Everybody I talk to says you're a user. A taker. But with your mother, you're the one who gets used."

"You better watch your mouth."

"Or what? You'll knock me off the shelf the way you did with your mother?"

Abel gaped.

"You didn't know who it was climbing up to you in the dark? I can't believe that. I think she came to you in the dark a lot."

It was all improvisation, and if she was wrong, Abel would put on his superior look, and the cops would never get another word out of him.

12

BUT SHE WASN'T wrong. She must have pressed a button, because Abel came at her over the table with a speed unlike anything she had ever encountered in five years of grappling with the toughest mokes on her island. She caught his wrist and turned it, but his adrenaline overrode whatever pain she was causing him.

The door banged open. She couldn't afford the time to look, but six hands joined her in forcing Abel down to the floor. Coutinho cuffed him, while Kenny and Sammy each bent a leg to immobilize him.

"You done?" Coutinho asked when his breathing permitted.

The young man didn't answer, but Coutinho took his silence for assent. He picked Abel up and dropped him on the chair he had occupied to begin with. But now he was a different young man, hunched and listless. Coutinho nodded at Jenny. She resumed her seat.

"So what happened?"

The silence stretched until she feared she had lost him. But he spoke in a trickle of words that would become a torrent.

"She found me that place."

"In the warehouse."

"Yeah. I knew it was her sneaking up on me. She must have wanted some."

"Some of what she had been taking from you all along?"

"Yeah. I know it's wrong. Now. But she started it a long time ago. It was a relief when she came here and left me in Vegas."

"But then she told you to come."

"Yeah."

He didn't need to add that he couldn't refuse his mother.

"Okay, your mother climbs up to your hideout and wakes you up."

"And all of a sudden I wasn't having it. Like, this is my new start, and she's trying to drag me back. I just gave her a shove. That's all it took. She never expected me to do it."

"So she fell. Did you check on her?"

"I just got out of there. I stepped right over her."

He didn't want to break down and ask, but his self-loathing wouldn't let him stop.

"Is she really dead?"

"If you want, I'll show you a picture from the morgue.

But I'm telling you the truth. No reason to put yourself through that."

"So I killed her."

Jenny had a decision to make. Which would get more out of him, the truth now, or letting him believe the worst for a while longer?

She knew the answer—whichever would make her feel worse.

"Did your mother know you killed Langston?"

"She could always read my mind."

"What did you hit him with?"

"The garden shears."

"Where are they?"

"Someplace in the neighborhood. I just walked away. At some point I realized I was carrying them. I just threw them into some bushes."

Coutinho would be on his phone to organize a search of the neighborhood, never mind how many previous searches had failed to turn the shears up.

It was still a big island.

Jenny went on.

"Why did you hit him?"

"The money. He was always hinting about it, but he would never say anything. He did it one time too many, and I just lost my shit over it."

Jenny thought about Abel's reputation in Las Vegas for cold savagery and ruthless calculation. This island had turned him into just another moke, all rage and reaction.

"You were never going to get it. Somebody else already had it."

That was sometimes how Jenny knew she had come to a conclusion. She listened to what came out of her mouth. She would have to talk it over with Coutinho, but right now she had more to say to Abel.

"You didn't kill your mother. She got up and got herself all the way to Hilo."

"Can I see her?"

"No. She survived the fall, but someone killed her. I'm sorry to have to tell you."

"Who?"

Jenny hesitated to reply. The old Abel was back, as if the death of his mother had cleared the deck in an instant. But it mattered less, now that he wasn't going anywhere but jail.

"Her friend Mrs. Conyers. You know her?"

"Now I know you're lying. She wouldn't even jaywalk."

Jenny tapped on her phone. There was no way the image could be anything but a booking photo, and the effect jarred Jenny, who had only known the woman for days. She could see how it shook Abel. His face remained a mask, but he shrank into himself.

"I'm sorry," she said. "It's hard, I know."

"I'm done talking," he said.

And a moke like him knew how to shut up. Jenny got up without a word. Coutinho and Cordova met her in the hall.

"That'll play in court," said the prosecutor.

They were standing there like three professionals who had done this before and would do it again. It would spoil the effect if Jenny launched into an end-zone celebration. She settled for nodding and making a date to high-five herself later over a beer.

Cordova went off down the hall. Coutinho turned to Jenny.

"We're sure about the money?"

"As sure as we can be."

●●●

Jenny badged her way into the boarding area beyond the security gate. The jurisdiction was federal if anybody wanted to make an issue of it, but the white shirted man from the sheriff's department just nodded her through.

The young man looked up at her with no expression that she could read.

"Where are you off to?"

"Vegas," said Caleb. "Wish I had more imagination about it."

"You can go anywhere you want. You're the last man standing."

"I'm not in the mood to get used to someplace new."

"Plus, you're in a position to buy some goodwill from the mob. Money heals all with them. So where did you find it?"

He gave her an expressionless look.

"I'm not the IRS," she said. "It won't make any difference if you tell me."

"How did you know I had it?"

"You've been off the island too long. In Vegas people deal in cash all the time. But here, somebody visiting bank after bank and depositing nine thousand dollars each time is going to get the *ohana* telegraph going."

He was still trying to stare her down.

"You know the term? *Ohana*? Family. Everybody here is related to everybody else. We talk. Better than a security camera on every block."

"You can't do anything about it," he said. "You can't prove the money is illegal."

"We know that."

"It was under the shrine. You know, the four stones. He buried a duffel bag and then piled up four stones on top of it like they were a shrine. Only they weren't."

Jenny thought about that. A few weeks of sub-tropical rains would have obliterated traces of Caleb's excavation.

Langston had probably needed several tries to find the right place. On this geologically new island, not every effort to dig a hole found sufficient depth in the soil. The mental picture came to Jenny of a troll hunkering obsessively over his treasure. What good had the money ever done him?

"That figures," she said. "Nobody would know the shrine wasn't real. Anyone local would just assume somebody else had built it, and they'd have left it alone. Only someone from the mainland would have messed with it, and Abel didn't think of looking there. Cindy didn't either. That left you."

Jenny would never know one thing—whether Langston had broken through the nearby skylight to the lava tube in his back yard while he was trying to dig a hole for his money. If that was the scenario, the goddess Pele had let it go once, but Langston hadn't heeded her warning.

Whenever I want you, you're mine.

"Be best if you didn't come back," she said.

The threat didn't come from her, but she didn't bother to explain about Pele. Caleb was too much of a mainlander to understand.

"Nothing here for me anyway," he said.

And that was the saddest thing an island dweller like Jenny had ever heard.

"Go," she said.

ACKNOWLEDGEMENT

To Fred and Debbie Tucher and my nephews Will and Dan for putting up with me during a dozen visits to Hawaii.

Photo Credit Mark Krajnak

ALBERT TUCHER is the creator of prostitute Diana Andrews, who has appeared in more than 100 hardboiled short stories in venues including *The Best American Mystery Stories 2010*, edited by Lee Child. Diana's first longer case, the novella *The Same Mistake Twice*, was published in 2013. Characters from her world figure in a new series set on the Big Island of Hawaii, which includes *The Place of Refuge*, *The Hollow Vessel*, *The Honorary Jersey Girl*, and *Blood Like Rain* all from Shotgun Honey.

Albert Tucher recently retired from the Newark Public Library, where he originally learned to drink too much coffee.

ABOUT SHOTGUN HONEY BOOKS

Thank you for reading *Pele's Prerogative* by Albert Tucher.

Shotgun Honey began as a crime genre flash fiction webzine in 2011 created as a venue for new and established writers to experiment in the confines of a mere 700 words. More than a decade later, Shotgun Honey still challenges writers with that storytelling task, but also provides opportunities to expand beyond through our book imprint and has since published anthologies, collections, novellas and novels by new and emerging authors.

We hope you have enjoyed this book. That you will share your experience, review and rate this title positively on your favorite book review sites and with your social media family and friends.

Visit ShotgunHoneyBooks.com

SHOTGUN HONEY
FICTION WITH A KICK

www.ingramcontent.com/pod-product-compliance
Lightning Source LLC
Chambersburg PA
CBHW011141190726
48289CB00012B/3105